MONSTERS WANTED
ARE YOU TALL?
ARE YOU GREEN?
ARE YOU SCARY?
IF YOU ANSWERED "YES" TO THOSE QUESTIONS, THEN COME WORK AT HORRORLAND THEME PARK!
IMPORTANT: HORRORLAND WILL ONLY HIRE MONSTERS WHO KNOW HOW TO KEEP SECRETS.
HorrorLand
www.EnterHorrorLand.com

MONSTERS
WANTED
ESCAPE
HORRORLAND
IF YOU ANSWERED "YES" TO THOSE QUESTIONS, THEN COME WORK AT HORRORLAND THEME PARK!
IMPORTANT: HORRORLAND WILL ONLY HIRE MONSTERS WHO KNOW HOW TO KEEP SECRETS.
HorrorLand

GOOSEBUMPS HorrorLand™
ALL-NEW, ALL-TERRIFYING

GOOSEBUMPS®
NOW WITH BONUS FEATURES!
LOOK IN THE BACK OF THE BOOK
FOR EXCLUSIVE AUTHOR INTERVIEWS AND MORE.

MY FRIENDS CALL ME MONSTER

R.L. STINE

SCHOLASTIC

Scholastic Children's Books
A division of Scholastic Ltd
Euston House, 24 Eversholt Street
London, NW1 1DB, UK
Registered office: Westfield Road, Southam, Warwickshire, CV47 0RA
SCHOLASTIC, GOOSEBUMPS, GOOSEBUMPS HORRORLAND, and
associated logos
are trademarks and/or registered trademarks of Scholastic Inc.

First published in the US in 2009 by Scholastic Inc.
This edition published in the UK by Scholastic Ltd, 2009
Goosebumps series created by Parachute Press, Inc.

ISBN 978 1407 10756 1

British Library Cataloguing-in-Publication Data.
A CIP catalogue record for this book is available from the British Library

Printed and bound by CPI Group (UK) Ltd, Croydon, CR0 4YY
Papers used by Scholastic Children's Books are made from wood grown in
sustainable forests.

12

This is a work of fiction. Names, characters, places, incidents and dialogues
are products of the author's imagination or are used fictitiously. Any
resemblance to actual people, living or dead, events or locales is entirely
coincidental.

www.scholastic.co.uk/zone

3 RIDES IN 1!

MY FRIENDS CALL ME MONSTER

"Michael, this is crazy," my friend Daisy Edwards whispered. "We shouldn't be here."

"Too late," I whispered back. "We're already here."

Daisy was right. Sneaking into our teacher's house was probably a bad idea.

But there we were, the three of us – me, Daisy and our friend DeWayne Walker – standing in Mrs Hardesty's kitchen. My eyes darted around, trying to see in the dim light. All the shades were pulled.

"Weird. She keeps her house as dark as our classroom," DeWayne said.

The kitchen smelled of cinnamon. Mrs Hardesty had a lot of snapshots on her fridge door. I glanced at them quickly. The faces all seemed blurry. An empty egg carton stood open on the sink.

I led the way into the front room. The shades were down there, too.

The sofa and four chairs all matched. They were black leather. I saw knitting needles sticking out of a ball of wool on a table beside the sofa. A tall wooden clock on the mantel ticked loudly.

"I'm not happy about this," Daisy whispered. "What if she comes home and finds us? We're *dead*!"

"No worries," I said. "She's still at school."

"Let's dump the cat and get *out* of here," DeWayne said. He raised the carrier in front of him. I could see the black cat's blue eyes peering out at me.

You're probably wondering why we sneaked into Mrs Hardesty's house with a black cat. Well, our plan was simple.

Mrs H is very superstitious. So . . . she comes home. She looks down and sees this black cat rubbing against her ankles . . . and it *totally* freaks her mind!

I wished I could be there when she went nuts. But I planned to be far, far away.

The cat pawed the front of the carrier and meowed. I think it wanted out.

"Monster, just open the carrier," DeWayne said. "Let it go, and we're *outta* here."

My friends call me Monster.

It's kind of a cool nickname. You see, I'm a big dude. I'm twelve, but I look like a high school guy. I'm pretty strong, too.

4

That's a *good* thing.

But I guess kids also call me Monster because of my temper. That's a *bad* thing.

My parents say I have a short fuse. That means I explode a lot. But, hey, I'm not angry *all* the time. Just when someone pushes my buttons.

Which is why my two friends and I were in Mrs Hardesty's house. Our teacher had been pushing my buttons ever since she arrived at Adams Middle School.

"Let the cat out," DeWayne said, holding the carrier up to my face.

"Not here," I said. "Mrs H will see it too soon. That's no fun."

"How about the basement?" Daisy said. "Mrs Hardesty opens the basement door, and there's a black cat at the bottom of the stairs, staring up at her. Can you picture it?"

"Awesome!" I said. I jabbed my finger into Daisy's forehead. "I like the way you think."

We searched the hall till we found the basement door. I pulled it open, and we stared down into the darkness. I fumbled for the light switch, and a bulb flashed on overhead.

I led the way down the creaky wooden steps. The cat meowed again. "Be patient," I said. "You'll have a nice, new basement to explore. And Mrs H will take good care of you."

We stepped into a short hallway. The air grew

cold and damp. The basement was divided into two rooms. Both doors were shut.

DeWayne set the carrier down on the floor. He bent to open its door.

That's when we heard the sound. A heavy *thump*. From one of the rooms.

We all froze. DeWayne's hands shot up, away from the carrier. He stared at me, his mouth open. Daisy took a step back.

I heard a groan. Another *thump*.

My heart did a flip-flop in my chest. "There's someone down here!" I whispered.

We didn't say another word. DeWayne grabbed the carrier by the handle, we spun away from the doors, and took off.

We scrambled up the stairs. Our trainers thudded loudly all the way up.

I was nearly at the top when I heard a metal *chiiing*. Something hit a stair and bounced down.

"Something fell out of my pocket!" I cried.

Was it my mobile phone?

I couldn't go back for it. We had to get out of there.

Someone – or some*thing* – was coming after us!

TWO WEEKS EARLIER

"How many of you have heard of the Loch Ness monster?" Mrs Hardesty asked. Several hands went up.

"Here she goes again," I whispered to DeWayne. He sat beside me in class.

DeWayne rolled his eyes. "Always monsters."

"The other sixth-grade class is doing the Civil War," I said. "All we talk about is monsters. How weird is that?"

DeWayne laughed. He's a lanky, good-looking dude. He wears low-riding, baggy jeans and long T-shirts with hip-hop singers across the front. He has big brown eyes and keeps his black hair shaved close to his head.

He's a good guy, except his laugh is too loud, which gets me in trouble a lot.

I suddenly realized Mrs Hardesty had her

beady little black eagle eyes on me. "Is something funny, Michael?" she asked.

I shrugged.

"Would you like to share it with the whole class?"

I shrugged again. "Whatever."

I should've just said *sorry* or something. Why do I always look for trouble with her?

Maybe because she's always on my case?

She stared at me with that cold expression, her face frozen like a statue.

Mrs Hardesty looks a lot like a bird, with tiny round eyes pushed up against a long beaky nose. She has short, feathery, white-blonde hair that puffs up around her pale narrow face.

"Would you care to tell the class what *you* think the Loch Ness monster looks like, Michael?"

"Well . . . it looks a lot like DeWayne, except it's prettier."

That got everyone laughing, except for Mrs Hardesty. She wrinkled her nose and made that sniffing sound she always makes when she's unhappy about something.

She held up a large photograph. "This is a photo of the Loch Ness monster," she said. She moved it from side to side, but it was really hard to see in the dim light.

She always keeps it dark in the room. Kids are always stumbling over their backpacks. When we take tests, we have to hold the paper up close to our faces to read it.

It was a bright, sunny day outside, but the shades were down and the ceiling lights were dim as usual.

"As you can see, the monster looks a lot like a dinosaur," Mrs Hardesty continued. "A lot of people claim this photo is a fake. People don't want to believe in monsters."

I reached into my jeans pocket and pulled out my silver dog whistle.

"But hundreds of people visit the lake in Scotland every year," Mrs H said. "They want to see the monster for themselves."

Kids gasped in surprise as one of the window shades shot up with a loud *snap*. Sunlight poured into the room.

Mrs Hardesty shielded her eyes. She edged sideways to the window and tugged the shade back down. The room grew dark again.

Mrs Hardesty picked up her lucky rabbit's foot from the desk. She always squeezes it in her hand when she gets tense. Which means she squeezes it a *lot*!

"Many other water monsters have been spotted over the centuries," she said. "In ancient times, sailors believed in sea serpents. And—"

SNAP.

The same window shade zipped back up to the top.

Mrs H gasped and dived to the window. She tugged it down and held it there for a few seconds. Then she returned to the front of her desk, rolling the rabbit's foot in her hand.

SNAP.

The shade flipped back up. Everyone laughed. Sunlight poured over the front of the room.

I hid the dog whistle under my desk. She hadn't seen me blow it. She had no idea what a mechanical genius Michael Munroe is.

Yeah, I'm real good with tech stuff. People don't expect it, because I'm Monster, the big hulk of a dude who is always getting into trouble.

But I've got a lot of skill with computers and all kinds of tech stuff.

Before class, I rigged the window shade. I put a tiny receiver on it. The dog whistle sent high-pitched sound waves to the receiver. Sound waves that humans can't hear. And the sound made the window shade go flying up.

SNAP.

I did it again. Just to upset Mrs H and get everyone laughing. Then I hid the whistle behind my textbook.

Mrs Hardesty scratched her head. "Why does that shade keep going up?" she asked.

"Maybe an *evil spirit* is doing it!" DeWayne said.

He knew I was doing it. But he liked to torture her, too. "*Owooooo.*" He made a nice ghost howl.

Mrs Hardesty's mouth dropped open. She didn't think it was funny. She was squeezing that lucky rabbit's foot *flat*!

"One should never joke about evil spirits," she said. Her voice trembled.

She kept a jar of black powder on her desk. She reached into the jar, pulled out a handful, and tossed it over her shoulder.

Is she the weirdest teacher on earth or *what*?

We're always trying to figure out what the black powder is. Daisy thinks it's ground-up bat wings. DeWayne says it's powdered eye of newt. He learned about eye of newt in one of the scary books he's always reading.

Mrs Hardesty tugged the window shade down and examined it carefully. I hoped she wouldn't spot the little receiver I'd planted there.

She returned to the front of the class. I raised my dog whistle and prepared to blow it again.

OOPS.

The whistle slipped out of my hand. I made a wild grab for it. But it bounced off my desk, hit the floor, and rolled halfway to Mrs Hardesty.

Did she see it?

Yes.

She squinted at it, then raised her eyes to me.

"Uh . . . am I in trouble?" I asked.

3

Yes, I was in trouble. She made me come back to class after school.

Outside, rain clouds covered the sky. That made the classroom even darker than before.

Mrs Hardesty had two tall white candles flickering on her desk. She was leaning over them, whispering to herself, when I dragged myself in.

"Mrs Hardesty, I'm sorry about the whistle thing," I said. "But I can't stay after school."

She kept whispering for a long while, her eyes shut. The candle smoke floated over her face, but she didn't seem to mind it.

Finally, she looked up at me. Her skin appeared grey and powdery in the candlelight. "Of course you will stay, Michael."

"No. Really," I said. "I can't. I'll miss wrestling practice."

Monster Munroe is the captain of the wrestling team. Who else?

"Sit down, Michael," Mrs H said. She pointed to a chair. "I want you to wrestle with your thoughts."

I let out a groan. "I can't go to practice?"

She reached into her jar and tossed a little black powder over her shoulder. "Sit down," she said.

I sat down. I threw my backpack angrily to the floor. I muttered some bad words under my breath.

I had that burning feeling in my chest. The feeling I get when someone is making me really mad.

Mrs Hardesty blew out the candles. She seemed to inhale the smoke. "Michael, do you think it's smart to make a fool of your teacher?" she asked.

"I really didn't have to try!" I blurted out.

OOPS. I did it again. Why can't I ever shut my trap?

I heard kids burst out laughing in the hall. I knew it was Daisy and DeWayne.

Mrs Hardesty leaped up from behind her desk. She strode to the classroom door and dragged my two friends in.

DeWayne plopped down next to me, shaking his head.

Daisy didn't look too happy, either. She never gets in trouble. She has this cute, innocent look. Curly carrot-coloured hair, lots of freckles, and dimples in her cheeks even when she isn't

13

smiling. So everyone thinks she's totally sweet and adorable.

Of course, I know better. I know she has a wicked-cold sense of humour. She could be a big problem child like me – if she put her mind to it.

"We didn't do anything," Daisy told Mrs Hardesty. "Why do we have to stay?"

The teacher waved for Daisy to sit down. Then she frowned at us one by one.

"You three need an attitude change," she said. She rubbed her pointed chin. "I think I know what will help."

"Me, too," I said. "Wrestling practice will help me. It'll change my attitude. Really."

DeWayne grinned at Mrs Hardesty. "I got an A in Attitude last term," he said. "You can check it out."

Mrs Hardesty rolled her eyes. "We don't grade for attitude," she muttered.

DeWayne squinted at her. "You sure?"

He was goofing on her. But she never got a joke.

"I know what will help you," Mrs H repeated. "Some honest work."

All three of us groaned.

"I'll give you a choice," she said. "You can stay two hours after school every day for a week."

We groaned again, louder.

"Or you can do some community service," Mrs H said.

We stared blankly at her. I had a sudden urge to take out my dog whistle and make the shade fly up again.

"I have a project that's perfect for you three," Mrs Hardesty said. "It's in the plot right by my house. You can come on Saturday."

"I can't," I said. "My dad is taking me to the big computer tech show. I—"

"I can't," Daisy said. "I have my tennis lesson, and—"

"Saturday," Mrs Hardesty insisted. "No excuses."

I heard a cough behind us. I turned and saw Mr Wong step into the room.

Mr Wong is our new principal. He's a little weird-looking. He's not old, but he has these sagging cheeks and bulging eyes that make him look like a frog. I'll bet his nickname was Froggy or Toadboy when he was a kid.

He wears dark pinstriped suits, white shirts and dark ties. He's a short dude. But he has a deep, booming voice. Kinda like a bullfrog.

But he's a good guy.

We never saw our old principal. She never came out of her office. Mr Wong is always out in the hall, greeting everyone and slapping high fives. He likes hanging out with us.

Mr Wong pulled Mrs Hardesty aside and asked what was going on. He kept glancing at the three of us. Mrs Hardesty had a frown on her face and kept pointing a long bony finger at me.

I couldn't hear everything they said. But I heard Mr Wong say, "I think you're being too hard on them. They were only having a little fun."

I told you. The Wongster is a good dude.

But Mrs Hardesty kept shaking her head, making her feathery hair bounce up and down. Finally, Mr Wong shrugged his shoulders and stepped back. Defeated.

Mrs Hardesty turned to us. "You three will show up for community service at two o'clock on Saturday. No excuses. We will meet at my house."

She walked back to her desk and started piling up papers.

Mr Wong walked up to us. "My house is right down the street from hers," he whispered. "I'll come out and check on how you're doing."

He turned and left the room.

The three of us started complaining to each other.

"Listen up," Mrs Hardesty said. "This is important. Be sure to wear work clothes on Saturday. And you'd better bring nose plugs."

Huh? *Nose plugs?*

What did she want us to *do* on Saturday?

4

Saturday was supposed to be totally fun. Dad had promised to take me to the computer tech show at the convention centre. I'd waited all year for this show.

But where was I on Saturday afternoon? Standing with Daisy and DeWayne behind Mrs Hardesty's house.

It was a warm, sunny day with a few white puffy clouds floating in a clear blue sky. But I didn't care.

I was really, really angry. I wanted to toss back my head and roar, and then start heaving things through Mrs Hardesty's window.

Instead, I followed my friends as Mrs H led us to the abandoned plot. The warm air started to smell – a really gross, sick smell. She stopped at a huge skip. A rubbish skip that stunk to high heaven.

"I need you to go through the rubbish,"

Mrs H said, "and pull out all the cans and bottles that can be recycled."

"Whoa!" DeWayne staggered back.

"Excuse me?" I said to Mrs H. "You want us to climb into the rubbish?"

"I thought I made it clear," she replied.

Daisy held her nose. She looked a little green.

"This is your community service," Mrs Hardesty said. "Climb in. Dig through the rubbish. Find all the cans, bottles and jars you can."

"But it *stinks*!" DeWayne cried. "It's putrid. It's sickening!"

Mrs Hardesty handed us each a long-handled shovel. "Good hunting," she said.

"But – but—" I sputtered.

She trotted back to her house.

Daisy, DeWayne and I stared at each other. Did we have a choice? I didn't think so.

A minute later, we were standing up to our knees in wet, putrid, slimy rubbish. The gunk soaked the legs of my jeans. The skunk-like aroma made my throat tighten up. I struggled not to choke.

I tried to walk. It was hard to balance. After a step or two, something squished under my trainer. A dead raccoon.

"I DON'T BELIEVE THIS!" I screamed. "This is totally UNFAIR!"

I lost it. I began to grab rubbish and heave it at the walls of the skip.

This wild picture flashed into my mind. I saw myself lifting the whole skip – like Superman – and emptying the rubbish into Mrs Hardesty's front window.

"NO WAY! NO WAAAAY!" I screamed, heaving rubbish all over the place.

Daisy grabbed one shoulder. DeWayne grabbed the other.

"Easy, Monster. Take it easy, dude," DeWayne said softly.

They were trying to hold me in place. But I lunged forward and broke free.

And fell face down into the wet rubbish.

I felt something ooze over my face. Something very wet and smelly soaked my T-shirt. I sat up on the skip floor, sputtering and shaking eggshells and rotten chunks of maggoty meat from my hair.

I tried to wipe the green, mouldy goop off my face, but it stuck there.

Finally, my friends pulled me to my feet.

DeWayne handed me my shovel. "Feeling better?"

I laughed. Suddenly, all three of us were laughing.

We started to shovel up rubbish. We didn't find many bottles or cans. Most people don't throw them in with the rubbish. But we kept searching through the yucky muck.

"Mrs Hardesty knew there wasn't much here to recycle," I said. "She put us in here just to be mean."

"*AAAIII!*" Daisy let out a scream. She started beating the rubbish frantically with the head of her shovel. "There's something ALIVE down there!" she wailed.

BAM! BAM! BAM!

Yes. She was right. Something down low in the skip was making the rubbish bubble up.

DeWayne and I grabbed Daisy, and we helped lower her from the skip. We followed her down to the ground and tossed our shovels away.

"Hey!" I let out a startled cry. Mr Wong was standing there.

Even though it was Saturday, he was dressed in one of his striped suits and a brown tie. His slicked-down black hair gleamed in the sunlight. His froggy eyes were soft and watery.

He had a smile on his face. But it disappeared when he saw the three of us covered in wet chunks of rubbish. He held his nose for a minute.

I didn't blame him. I could smell myself. Believe me, it wasn't pretty.

"Nice job, guys," he said, still holding his nose. "Here. I brought you candy bars. For energy." He handed us each a chocolate bar.

20

Then he pulled out a wad of paper towels from his jacket pocket. "Here. You can wipe some of the rubbish off."

We thanked him. He hurried away, running, not walking. Our smell was making him feel sick.

I used a paper towel to wipe sticky stuff off my forehead. My jeans and T-shirt were soaked through and stained. My back itched. Rubbish bugs had climbed under my shirt.

Daisy and DeWayne were muttering to each other. I couldn't hear them. My ears were ringing. That happens a lot when I'm really angry.

"I'm going to take a two-hour shower," DeWayne said.

Daisy pulled a brown hunk of lettuce from her hair. The lettuce was covered with tiny brown worms.

"The next time my mom asks me to take out the rubbish, I'll probably go berserk," she said.

I clenched my teeth. I stared at Mrs Hardesty's house. "I'm going to pay her back," I said. "This was totally mean and unfair. I'm going to find a way to pay her back."

But how?

We said goodbye. We headed off in different directions to our houses.

I was slinking home through back gardens. Trying to stay in the shadows. I didn't want anyone to see me. Or smell me!

21

I saw something move. I stopped. Between two houses – a black cat. It was sitting very still now, staring at me with big blue eyes.

More bad luck?

No. No way. Suddenly, I knew just how I was going to get my revenge.

And that's how Daisy, DeWayne and I ended up sneaking into Mrs Hardesty's house with the black cat.

My two friends didn't really want to do it. Sneaking into a teacher's house is kind of scary. But it didn't take much to convince them.

Daisy had shampooed her hair ten times. But it still had bugs crawling in it. And DeWayne said he had to throw out his jeans and T-shirt. His mother refused to wash anything that smelly.

So we all had a good reason for getting even with Mrs Hardesty.

We knew how superstitious she was. She talked all the time about how black cats really do bring bad luck. She told us that once you have the bad luck, it's hard to shake it off.

So what could be better?

A black cat suddenly appears in her basement. And she FREAKS. She totally freaks!

The black cat was always around our neighbourhood. No one knew who it belonged to. I think it had a *hundred* and nine lives! I saw it wherever I went.

So we gathered up the cat and hurried to Mrs Hardesty's house after school. We knew she was staying late for some parent meetings. We made sure her blue car wasn't in the driveway. And none of the neighbours were watching.

The back door was unlocked. We walked right into the kitchen.

Down to the basement. We tried to be as silent as possible. The cat kept pacing back and forth inside the carrier.

We planned to be fast. Get in. Free the cat. Get out.

But it didn't work that way.

We heard thumps and moans and groans coming from one of the rooms. My heart did a flip-flop in my chest.

Someone else was down there.

We stumbled up the stairs as fast as we could. Something fell out of my jeans pocket, but I didn't go back for it. The cat was meowing like crazy.

We made it back upstairs, breathing hard. Were we being chased?

I turned and stared down into the dark basement. No. No one on the stairs.

I gripped the basement door and leaned against it, waiting for my heart to stop pounding. "It's OK," I finally said. "We're OK."

Daisy glanced around. "Let the cat out," she told DeWayne. "And let's go."

DeWayne set the carrying case on the floor. He reached for the clasp.

"No. Wait," I said. "The attic. Let's take it up to the attic."

They both squinted at me. "Why?"

"It'll be scarier," I said. "Think about it. Mrs H is sitting in the living room. She hears something creeping down the attic stairs. She opens the attic door – and there is BAD LUCK staring her in the face!"

I laughed. I could just picture it.

DeWayne shook his head. "Monster, you are *too bad*!" he said.

"Too stupid," Daisy muttered. "I can't believe I'm doing this. If we get caught. . ." She shivered, then hugged herself.

"We won't get caught," I said. I glanced out the front window. No sign of the teacher's car. "You know how long those parent meetings take. We have all afternoon."

We had to explore a little to find the attic steps. The door stood at the end of the hall next to Mrs Hardesty's bedroom.

We opened the door. The attic was pitch-black.

25

As we climbed, the air grew warmer. It smelled stale, kind of musty.

The cat thumped the side of the carrier. It was eager to get out.

I stepped into the attic. It was huge. The walls were knotty pine. Two tiny windows faced the front. They let in narrow beams of light.

The attic was filled with furniture covered with sheets. An old typewriter and a black plastic radio sat on a wooden crate. A long brown leather sofa stood sideways in the middle of the floor. The sheet had fallen off one side of it.

Something big and tall and almost round stood near us at the top of the stairs. It was totally covered by a sheet. It was at least six feet tall. What could it be? Some kind of sculpture?

I started to lift the sheet to take a peek. But Daisy pulled me away. "No time to sightsee," she whispered. "It's hot up here. Let's hurry."

DeWayne set the carrier down in front of the long sofa. He opened the front.

The cat stepped out quickly. It took three or four steps, then stretched its legs, tilting its head from side to side. It glanced around the long room for a few seconds. Then it just stood there, staring up at us with its blue eyes.

"Mission accomplished," I said. "This is way perfect. I can't wait—"

That's when I heard the car door slam outside.

My mouth dropped open. I saw Daisy's eyes go wide. The three of us froze. So did the cat!

I dived to one of the tiny windows and peered down at the driveway.

I groaned. "Oh, wow. It's Mrs Hardesty! She's home."

DeWayne looked ill. Daisy let out a cry. "How do we get *out* of here?"

I watched Mrs H step up to her front door.

"We're kinda trapped," I said.

We heard the front door open and close. We heard Mrs Hardesty step into the front hall.

She coughed. Muttered something to herself.

I could hear every sound. It was as if I suddenly had super hearing skills!

"If she catches us, we're dead meat," Daisy whispered.

DeWayne swallowed. "Think we'll be suspended from school?"

"She'll probably put us in front of a firing squad," Daisy said.

"Bad attitude," I said. "We'll get out of this."

I always try to look on the bright side. Even when I'm *doomed*!

I gazed around the attic. No back door. No escape route. If we started down the stairs now, she'd see us.

Could we climb out a window and lower ourselves to the ground?

No. The windows were too small.

I waved the others behind the long sofa. We crouched down on our hands and knees.

Where was the cat?

I poked my head out and searched. No sign of it. Was it already heading down the stairs?

That could be trouble.

I pressed my side against the back of the sofa and listened. I couldn't hear Mrs Hardesty. The only sound I heard was my own heavy breathing.

Then I heard water running. Probably from the kitchen sink?

It stopped. I could hear Mrs Hardesty humming to herself. Then I heard footsteps growing louder.

"She's coming upstairs," Daisy whispered. "Probably to her bedroom. To change out of her school clothes."

DeWayne sniggered. "Do teachers have school clothes?"

"*Shhhh.*" Daisy gave DeWayne a shove. "Want her to hear you?" she whispered.

More footsteps. Mrs Hardesty coughed again. The sound floated up the attic stairs.

She was too close, *too close* to us now.

One sound, and she'd know someone was up there.

I held my breath. All three of us froze.

That's when the cat decided to meow. A long, shrill cry.

I gasped and shut my eyes.

Doomed. Doomed!

I opened my eyes and saw the cat sitting beside me.

"*Shhhh,*" I whispered. Do cats understand what *shhhh* means?

I wrapped both arms around the cat and pulled it close to my chest. I held it there, praying it wouldn't make another sound.

"*Meeeeeeeeeeeew!*"

Another long howl.

I gritted my teeth. DeWayne shut his eyes and crouched with his hands raised in a praying position. Daisy stared straight ahead.

And we heard footsteps. The attic stairs creaked. The footsteps were coming closer.

We were caught. Mrs Hardesty was climbing the attic stairs.

7

I hugged the cat even closer to my chest. "Please," I whispered. "Please be quiet."

The attic stairs creaked and groaned. Keeping low, I poked my head out just enough to see.

Mrs Hardesty climbed into the attic.

Daisy was right. She had changed her clothes. She was wearing a grey sweatshirt over baggy purple trousers. Instead of her black pumps, she wore black trainers.

Please don't meow. Please don't make a sound, I silently begged the cat.

Mrs Hardesty glanced around. She took a few steps towards the sofa.

She wiped something off the old radio with one hand. Then she moved to a window and peered down at the street.

Was it the longest, scariest moment of my life?

Yes. But I knew it would get a lot scarier if our teacher caught us there.

I heard voices. Some kids playing outside. I wished I was out there with them.

I hugged the cat tighter. Was I smothering the poor thing?

Mrs Hardesty moved away from the window. She stepped up to the tall covered thing by the stairs.

Still hugging the cat to my chest, I peeked out from behind the sofa.

She was pulling the sheet off. After a few seconds, I could see a little bit of what was underneath. It was smooth and white.

She tugged the sheet away and folded it neatly. I stared at what she had uncovered. Stared at it in disbelief.

It was an egg. A six-foot-tall egg.

Daisy and DeWayne were crouched beside me behind the sofa. They couldn't see what I was seeing. They stared straight ahead, afraid to breathe.

Mrs Hardesty walked around the egg a few times, inspecting it. She smoothed her hand gently over the shell as she circled it.

She had a strange smile on her face. Her eyes sparkled with excitement.

What kind of bird or animal could lay an egg that big? I asked myself.

A few weeks earlier, I had seen dinosaur eggs on a cool show on the Discovery Channel. They were *tiny* compared to this giant egg.

It can't be real, I decided. *It's a sculpture. Yes. That's it. It's a piece of art.*

Someone made it out of plaster or something. That's why Mrs Hardesty was acting so proud of it.

While those thoughts whirred through my mind, Mrs H stopped circling. She faced the egg and stretched both arms around its wide middle.

Was she *hugging* it?

No.

I gasped as she pulled herself off the floor. Her trainers pushed against the eggshell. She slid her hands higher . . . higher. . .

And in seconds, she had climbed to the top. Then she turned to face the window. *She was sitting on top of the egg!*

Wow. That shell must be really thick and tough, I thought.

I watched her settle herself up there. She lowered her hands beside her on the shell.

Daisy and DeWayne had to see this. Otherwise, they'd think I was making it up.

Silently, I crawled backwards and made a space for them. Then I waved for them to move and take a look.

They didn't make a sound. They poked their heads around the side of the sofa. I saw their eyes bulge in shock. They both shook their heads, totally bewildered.

33

I pushed them back so I could see again. My head was spinning.

What on earth was our teacher doing up there? Was she *hatching the egg*?

What would come bursting out of it? A giant CHICKEN?!?

How weird is this?

She stared out the window. Her hands rested on top of the egg. Her trainers dangled three feet off the floor. She seemed very comfortable up there.

We have to get out of here!

That thought repeated in my brain.

But how?

I was still holding the cat. I glanced down. It had fallen asleep in my arms. Sweet.

The cat was one thing I didn't have to worry about – for now. How long would Mrs H sit on that egg? Till dinner time? Even later?

I settled against the back of the sofa. I set the cat down on the floor. Then I crossed my arms and waited. My friends didn't move, either. I think it was the longest we'd ever sat still.

The longest day of my life!

Time passed so slowly. The afternoon sun turned red as it lowered in the attic windows. I could see the evening sky and a pale, white half-moon in the skylight above us.

I heard a sound. A soft snore.

I peeked around the edge of the sofa. *Yes!*

Mrs H was still sitting on top of the egg. But her head was down and she was snoring softly.

"She's asleep," I whispered to my friends.

They both sat forward. Their eyes went wide. DeWayne stretched his arms over his head.

"Think we can sneak past her?" Daisy whispered.

"It's our only chance," I said.

"If we wake her up. . ." DeWayne's voice trailed away.

I knew it was going to be tough. We had to walk right past the egg to get to the attic stairs.

One little sound . . . one quick move could wake Mrs Hardesty.

And then we'd be caught standing there – *seeing* her. Seeing her hatching a giant egg!

What would she *do* to us?

"Take off your shoes," I whispered. "Don't make a sound."

Leaning against the sofa back, we tugged off our trainers. Then, carrying them in front of us, we tiptoed towards the stairs.

I led the way, taking one step at a time.

The floor squeaked under my foot. I stopped, my eyes on Mrs Hardesty. She didn't raise her head.

I realized I wasn't breathing. I sucked in a deep breath and held it. Then I continued creeping slowly forward, one step at a time.

It seemed to take hours. Finally, I was standing in front of the egg. Mrs Hardesty's knees were inches from my face. Two more steps and I would reach the top of the stairs.

One. . .

Two. . .

And a hand grabbed me hard by the shoulder!

I gasped and froze. I turned my head.

Daisy!

"S-sorry," she whispered. "I started to trip."
Her hand slid from my shoulder.

My heart was still doing a four-minute mile!

On top of the egg, Mrs Hardesty let out a soft
murmur. Was she waking up?

Leaning on the banister, I flew down the stairs
without looking back. I reached the hall, ran past
Mrs Hardesty's bedroom, and kept going. I heard
my two friends close behind me.

We stopped at the kitchen door and listened.
No sounds from upstairs. Maybe Mrs H was still
sleeping.

We burst outside into the cool evening air. The
sun was nearly down, just a red stripe behind
the houses. The trees fluttered in gusts of wind.

We didn't say a word. We ran through several
back gardens, then an empty plot.

I stopped running at the traffic light on the

corner of my street. I pressed my hands against my knees, waiting to catch my breath.

DeWayne kept glancing behind him. The air was cold, but his face was drenched with sweat. "What should we do now?" he asked.

"We have to tell someone what we saw," Daisy said. She gripped a street light. She looked pale in the white light. All of her freckles had disappeared.

"Who can we tell?" I asked, standing up. I felt a little dizzy. "And what could we say? That we saw Mrs Hardesty hatching a giant egg?"

"Think people would laugh at us?" DeWayne asked.

"Yeah. I think so," I said.

"We should tell Mr Wong," Daisy said. "He'd listen to us."

"He'd listen to us," I said. "But he wouldn't believe us. I'm not sure *I* believe it!"

We stared at each other. A dark car rolled past with loud music blasting out the windows. Kids waved to us from the back. We didn't wave back.

"Let's go home and just think about this," DeWayne said.

Daisy shuddered. "I won't be able to think about anything *else*!" she said.

"Wait! I've *got* it!" DeWayne cried. He tapped his head. "The Great Brain strikes again!"

I squinted at him. "What have you got?" I asked.

"I can explain it," he said. "I can explain everything."

"Spill," Daisy said. She turned to me. "This should be good."

"Mrs Hardesty saw us," DeWayne said. "She knew we were hiding behind the sofa. So she climbed up on the egg and pretended to be hatching it *just to freak us out.*"

I shook my head. "It was all a joke? Then explain this: why does she have a giant egg in her attic? In case some kids sneak up there and hide behind her sofa?"

"And why did she fall asleep if she was goofing on us?" Daisy asked. "And why did she let us get away so easily?"

DeWayne shrugged. "Do you think I know *everything?*"

My stomach growled. "Let's go home," I said. "We're late for dinner. Let's go home and think about this. Catch you later."

We headed off in different directions.

Mom greeted me at the kitchen door. "Michael, you're so late," she said. "Where were you?"

"Uh . . . wrestling practice," I said.

I got to school a little late the next morning. I dumped my jacket in my locker and looked for

Daisy and DeWayne. No sign of them. I guessed they were already in class.

"Yo, Monster!" A guy from the wrestling team flashed me a thumbs up.

I turned a corner – and bumped into Mr Wong. He was in his usual pinstriped suit. But today he wore a bright red tie. Very bold.

"Michael, what's up?" he asked, grinning at me. "How are things going?"

Should I tell him?

"My friends and I saw something way weird, Mr Wong. We saw Mrs Hardesty climb up on a giant egg and try to hatch it."

No. No way. I couldn't say it.

"Things are OK, I guess," I said.

He was so short, he reached up to put a hand on my shoulder. "If you have any problems, you come to me," he said. "And we'll talk about it, OK? My door is always open."

I nodded. "Thanks," I muttered. I didn't know what else to say.

He hurried away. I stood there and watched him bounce down the hall.

Weird, I thought. *Does he suspect that something is wrong with Mrs Hardesty? Is that why he said that to me?*

I started to walk into class. But Mrs Hardesty stopped me at the door.

She led me back into the hall and closed the door behind us. Her tiny round eyes stared into mine.

"Is anything wrong?" I asked. I tried to keep my voice calm and normal.

She didn't answer. Just kept staring at me.

I gazed right back at her. If she wanted a staring contest, I was up for it. I've never lost a staring contest in my life. I once stared so long and hard at DeWayne, he went cross-eyed!

"I found something in my house last night," Mrs H said finally.

She blinked. I won the contest.

"I found a black cat in my bedroom," she said. Her teeth were clenched tight. Her cheeks turned red.

"Really?" I said. "Black cats are bad luck, aren't they?"

Was she buying my innocent act?

"I stayed up all night, Michael," she said. "All night, trying to rid my house of the bad luck."

I didn't reply.

She brought her face close to mine, so close I could smell the coffee on her breath. "Did you have anything to do with that, *Michael*?" she asked. She said my name as if it was something disgusting.

I backed up against the tile wall. She kept her face right above mine.

"Michael? Tell me the truth. Did you have something to do with bringing that bad-luck cat into my house?"

"No way," I said. "Of course not."

Her eyes – cold as ice – sent a chill rolling down my back.

She is dangerous, I decided.

Why was she standing so close? Why was she staring so hard?

Was she trying to read my mind?

I have to tell someone about her, I thought. *I have to get proof so they will believe me.*

I have to find out what she's hatching in her attic.

I suddenly realized I had no choice. I had to sneak back up to that attic to see what came crawling out of that egg.

"No way," Daisy said.

"Ditto," DeWayne said.

I had to chase them down the street. "You won't come back to the attic with me?"

"Do I look like I'm crazy?" Daisy asked. "Don't answer that."

"Monster, it's not our business," DeWayne said. "If Mrs H wants to hatch giant chickens in her attic, that's her problem."

"But – but—" I sputtered.

I couldn't believe my friends were refusing to come along with me. "*You're* the giant chickens!" I said.

They both nodded. "You got that right," DeWayne said.

"But don't you want to know the truth?" I asked. "Don't you want to be able to prove to people how crazy she is?"

DeWayne lifted two fingers to his ear. "Call

me," he said. "Call me later and tell me what you found."

"Yeah. Call me, too," Daisy said. "Long distance. I'm never going near that house again."

They trotted away.

Which is why I ended up in Mrs Hardesty's attic that afternoon all by myself.

The back door was unlocked, just like before. I sneaked into the house and made my way up to the attic without stopping.

I didn't see any sign of the black cat. It was probably back outside, prowling the neighbourhood.

Dark storm clouds hung low in the sky. The attic was even darker than before. I stood beside the egg, waiting for my eyes to adjust.

Should I lift the sheet?

I wanted to feel the egg. Was it warm or cold? Did it feel like a regular eggshell? Could I feel a giant chicken growing inside it?

I gripped the sheet and started to pull.

No.

I changed my mind. Mrs Hardesty might notice that it was moved.

I let go of the sheet and crossed the room. Dropping down behind the sofa, I prepared to wait.

This time, I had brought two chocolate bars so I wouldn't starve.

I was half finished with the second bar when I heard a car door slam out in the driveway. A few seconds later, I heard the front door open and close.

My heart started to pound. My hands were suddenly cold and sweaty.

I jammed the rest of the chocolate bar into my backpack. Then I pressed my back against the sofa and made myself comfortable.

After a short while, I heard Mrs Hardesty climb the stairs to her room. She was in there a long time. I could hear her walking around.

Maybe she isn't coming up to the attic today, I thought.

Maybe I sneaked up here for nothing.

But no. After a few more minutes, I heard the attic door open. Then I heard Mrs Hardesty's footsteps on the creaking wooden stairs.

I stayed frozen behind the sofa until she stepped into the attic. Then I poked my head out just enough to see her.

She had changed into the same grey sweatshirt and loose-fitting purple trousers. She had her back to me. She was tugging the sheet off the egg.

She folded it up and set it aside on the floor. Then, once again, she circled the egg slowly, running her open hand along the fat middle of the shell.

I kept blinking in the grey light of the attic. I

still couldn't believe what I was seeing!

Will she hatch the egg today?

Will it EVER hatch?

I had this sudden impulse. A crazy thought.

I pictured myself climbing out from behind the sofa. Walking over to her. Very casual-like. My hands in my pockets. A big smile on my face.

And I'd say, "Hey, Mrs H, what's up with that big egg? What've you got goin' on there?" And then I'd click a photo with my mobile phone.

Luckily, I held myself back.

I mean, a dude could get in trouble for sneaking into a teacher's house – especially if the teacher had a big secret to keep.

So I stayed on my hands and knees. Kept myself as low to the floor as possible. And I stared in silence as my teacher climbed the egg once again and perched on top.

She sat up there a long time without moving. I didn't move, either.

My arms were getting sore, and my neck felt stiff.

Raindrops pattered the roof, and I heard thunder in the distance. The sky darkened to black, and the blackness seeped into the attic.

I hunched there, squinting through the dim light. Watching . . . waiting . . . watching.

My head jerked back when I heard the loud *crack*.

My muscles tightened. I blinked several times, trying to wake myself up.

Another *craaaack*. Louder this time.

Mrs Hardesty's eyes bulged, and a smile spread over her face. She turned her body around. Wrapped her arms around the shell. And slid down to the floor.

CRAAAACK.

Mrs Hardesty pumped her fists in the air. She let out a happy cheer. I could see that she was very excited.

I heard more cracking sounds. Some soft thuds. A *tap-tap-tap* sound like a hammer against wood.

A tiny wedge of the shell poked open and fell to the floor.

I held my breath. It was so hard to stay still. This was the big moment!

Another long *CRAAAAACK.*

Another section of eggshell dropped off the egg. I could see yellow yolky stuff inside.

And then . . . then. . .

I slapped my hand over my mouth to keep from making a sound.

And I stared in shock as a glistening, wet green arm poked out of the egg. Dripping with yolk slime, the scaly arm stretched itself out, then curled and uncurled its pointed claw.

47

I couldn't breathe. I couldn't blink.

The shell cracked open. Yellow goo drained on to the floor and formed a wide puddle at Mrs Hardesty's feet.

She had this strange smile frozen on her face. Her eyes flashed with excitement.

As I stared in shock, she grabbed the wet green arm. Gently, she wrapped her fingers around its bony claw – and tugged.

I almost screamed as the creature came tumbling out of the egg.

It was big – as big as my neighbour's Labrador retriever!

It had bumpy green skin covered in thick slime, like a layer of yellow mucus. The skin reminded me of alligator skin. Or maybe lizard skin.

"UNNNNNH. UNNNNNH."

It made loud, disgusting choking noises as it tried to breathe. It opened up its long snout and coughed up huge balls of yellow snot.

Its round black eyes rolled crazily in its thin lizardy head. *"UNNNH. UNNNNH."* It coughed up more snot balls and sent them plopping at Mrs Hardesty's feet.

The creature stood awkwardly on its hind legs. The legs were short, like alligator legs. But the creature had a long bumpy body. And a large smooth head with a long snout.

It stretched its front legs out. It curled and uncurled its claws. Its slime-covered head tilted and turned as it gazed around the attic.

Then, with a hoarse cry, it stumbled back into the shell.

Mrs Hardesty reached out both hands and tugged it out on to its feet.

The creature opened its long snout and whimpered. Like a baby!

This isn't happening, I told myself.

I'm not hunched here on my hands and knees in my teacher's attic, watching her hatch a giant green monster!

"UNNNNH. UNNNNNH." It tossed back its head and uttered more choking sounds.

"Easy, my little baby," Mrs Hardesty said softly. "Easy. Let Mama help you."

She picked up a bath towel and began to wipe the thick mucus off the creature's back. "There, there, little baby."

Little baby?!

She was very gentle with it. It took four towels to wipe all the sticky goo off its body. She carefully wiped its legs, its claws and its tiny black nails.

It *oohed* and *cooed* as she towelled it down. It snapped its jaws in the air. Testing them out, I guess. I couldn't believe it. It already had teeth!

"Stand still, my little baby," Mrs Hardesty whispered. She gently plucked a big piece of eggshell off the monster's back. Then she towelled it some more.

She petted its smooth head for a minute or two and talked baby talk to it.

I almost *puked* when she said, "OK, little baby, give Mama a kiss."

A snaky black tongue slid out of its mouth. Mrs Hardesty leaned forward – and gave the creature a big . . . wet . . . KISS! *Smack smack.*

Ohhhh, gross!

Could it be any more sick?

"You're going to be a good boy," Mrs Hardesty said. She petted its head some more. "You love your mama – don't you! You're not like those nasty students."

Oh, wow. I didn't want to hear any more of it. I wanted to get out of there. I was desperate to tell everyone what was going on here.

My arms and legs were numb from not moving all that time. My back ached. My brain was spinning.

I peeked out from behind the sofa. Mrs Hardesty had the monster by the claw. She tugged it forward slowly.

She was guiding it down the attic stairs.

"*UNNNNH.*" It coughed up a snot ball and sent it sailing on to the wall. Its legs moved awkwardly. Its big body bumped the stair railing.

Where was she taking it?

They were climbing down the stairs one at a time. When her head disappeared from view, I crawled out from my hiding place.

Did I dare follow her? I had to. I had to know where she planned to keep the thing.

I got to my feet. My legs were totally numb. I stretched, trying to get my blood flowing again.

Silently, I tiptoed to the stairs.

I held my breath. Moving slowly, carefully, I began to follow them.

"I've GOT you!" Mrs Hardesty cried.

11

I gasped – and grabbed the banister to keep from falling.

It took me several seconds to realize she was talking to the baby monster. Not to me.

I forced myself to breathe again. I waited for my heart to stop pounding against my chest.

They were out of my sight, already in the first-floor hallway.

I made my way down the attic stairs and peered into the hall. She was leading it down to the ground floor.

The monster was walking more steadily now. Mrs Hardesty gripped its claw in one hand and kept talking gently to it. I couldn't hear what she was saying. I knew it was probably more goo-goo baby talk.

Yucko.

I stayed back, waiting for them to go down the stairs. I pressed myself against the wall and hid in the shadows.

Finally, it was safe to move again. By the time I reached the kitchen, Mrs Hardesty was already taking the monster downstairs. To the basement.

I stepped into the doorway. The basement stairs were dark. But if she turned around, she'd see me.

She didn't turn around.

I remembered that her basement was divided into two rooms. She took the monster to the door on the right. She fumbled around in her trouser pocket, then pulled out a key.

I crept down one step. Then one more.

I couldn't get too close. But I had to see what she was doing with the creature.

I tried one more step. It squeaked loudly under my feet.

I froze.

Did Mrs Hardesty hear it?

No. She unlocked the door and pulled it open.

Oh, wow. I saw a dimly lit room. And . . . and . . . at least a *dozen* green monsters. All of them stood on their hind legs. All of them turned to watch Mrs Hardesty bring in the new baby.

Mrs Hardesty stepped into the room. They lumbered forward to greet her, grunting and mewing.

"Hello, my babies! My cute babies!" she exclaimed.

Cute babies?

They were even taller than Mrs Hardesty. Their dark green bodies were scaly and lizardy. Their jaws snapped excitedly.

"How are all my little babies?" Mrs Hardesty asked. She used a tender voice I'd never heard in class.

The monsters formed a circle around her. One of them stuck its black snake tongue out and licked her face.

She laughed. "Sweet! Sweet!"

Then her smile faded. "Soon, I will not have to hide you away down here," she told them. "Soon, there will be more of US than of THEM!"

What was she talking about? More MONSTERS than HUMANS?

A chill ran down my back. What was she planning to do with these monsters she was hatching?

"I made a promise to Commander Xannx," Mrs Hardesty said. "We will succeed in our mission. We will take over this planet. And we will TRIUMPH over the weak Earthlings!"

I shook my head hard. This was too disturbing.

It was like I couldn't take it all in. I recognized all the words she said, but they didn't make sense to me.

She couldn't be saying what I thought she was saying.

Was Mrs Hardesty an alien? From another planet? Sent here by some alien commander with a name no human could pronounce?

And was she planning a war – monsters against humans?

No. Please – no.

If it was true, I was the only human on Earth who knew about it. The only human on Earth who could stop her.

But, whoa. Wait. I'm big and I'm strong – but I'm just a twelve-year-old kid.

If I was going to stop Mrs Hardesty and her monster war, I was gonna need HELP. A *lot* of help!

I stared into the room. The monsters had closed in on Mrs Hardesty. One of them was licking her face. Another green scaly beast was licking the back of her hand. Two of them had their front legs around her shoulders and were hugging her.

And she kept cooing to them and saying, "My babies . . . my babies."

I had to get away from there. I had to tell someone. *Everyone!*

The main thing was to escape this house without being caught.

I turned. I gripped the banister. I started to climb the stairs.

I made it up three steps – and then I couldn't help it. I SNEEZED.

12

Caught.

There was *no way* she didn't hear that.

It wasn't a quiet sneeze. I never learned how to sneeze quietly.

I swallowed hard and held my breath. I stood there with one foot on one step, the other beneath it on a lower step.

I froze there – every muscle tensed – and shut my eyes. And waited for her to call me down there.

But no.

I heard her gooey-sweet voice. "Does one of my babies have a cold?"

I let my breath out slowly. She thought one of the monsters had sneezed!

. I turned back to the room. Through the open door, I saw Mrs Hardesty walk to a refrigerator against the back wall. "Are my babies hungry? Are you ready for din-din?"

This got them all excited. They began huffing

and puffing and jumping up and down. Two of them got into a headbutting contest. Each time their heads collided, it made a wet *smack*.

Mrs Hardesty pulled open the fridge door and leaned inside. She came out with big hunks of red, raw meat.

She tossed the meat chunks high in the air. They landed on the floor. The excited monsters dived head first for them.

They scrambled for the meat. Head-butted and shoved and tackled each other out of the way.

The *smack* of their bodies rang out over the sick gobbling and slurping. They sucked the meat chunks into their open mouths and swallowed them whole. Then they tossed back their heads, opened their mouths wide, and let out deafening, two- and three-minute burps.

As the monsters devoured the meat, Mrs Hardesty stepped to the side. She crossed her arms in front of her and watched. She had an adoring smile pasted on her face. She actually thought these slobbering, burping beasts were *cute*!

A few minutes later, the meat was gone. The last monster finished his roaring burp. The basement room grew quiet.

Mrs Hardesty stepped forward. "OK, my babies," she said. "Listen up now. I want you to lay more eggs."

The creatures stood at attention, their eyes locked on her. A short chubby one made a gurgling noise and vomited up his meat on to the floor. He bent down and quickly ate it a second time.

"Lay more eggs!" Mrs H told them. "We will use some of them to hatch more babies. And I will feed some of the eggs to the kids at my school. Then to the whole *town*! And then – monsters rule! Monsters rule! *Monsters rule!*"

Her chant got the monsters all psyched. They nodded their heads up and down. They danced as if getting ready for battle. A few of them did some more headbutting.

"The Commander will be proud!" Mrs Hardesty shouted, pumping a fist in the air. "We will take over this puny planet – or my name isn't Hyborg-Xrxuz!"

The monsters were pumped. They roared and hopped up and down.

"Oh, wow," I murmured. "Oh, wow."

Mrs Hardesty wasn't really Mrs Hardesty. She had a weird alien name – *because she was an alien*!

An alien who came to Earth to get rid of humans and make a home for these ugly monsters.

I spun around and ran up the basement stairs as fast as I could. The monsters were making such a racket down there, I knew Mrs H couldn't hear me.

My legs felt rubbery and weak. My heart was thumping in my chest.

But I ran out the back door and kept running.

I had to tell everyone. I had to *warn* everyone. We were *all* in danger.

A horn honked and tyres squealed as I ran across the street. I hadn't even looked to see if anyone was coming. I heard the driver shout at me from his open window. But I didn't stop.

The houses and gardens were a blur. I ran all the way home. Mrs Hardesty's cheer rang in my ears: "Monsters rule! Monsters rule!"

I saw her pumping her fist in the air as the monsters bounced up and down. "Monsters rule! Monsters rule!"

No way! I told myself.

I burst in through the back door. Mom and Dad were standing in the kitchen. Dad was chopping onions at the table. His face was red, and tears rolled down his cheeks. Mom was stirring a pot on the stove.

They turned when I came roaring in.

"Michael, where have you been?" Dad asked through his tears.

I struggled to catch my breath. "I was at Mrs Hardesty's," I choked out. "Mom! Dad! She's hatching big green monsters. She keeps them in her basement. She's going to turn everyone in town into monsters!"

Dad set down the onions. He blinked at me. "That's pretty serious, Michael," he said. "Let's get the police over there and put an end to this!"

13

Dad's onion tears rolled down his cheeks, and he laughed.

Mom laughed, too.

I stood there still breathing hard, my legs trembling. I gritted my teeth and watched them laugh at me.

"Michael, we know you don't like your teacher," Mom said finally. "And yes, I'll admit she's a little *different*. . ."

"But there's no point in making up crazy stories about her," Dad said.

Mom tapped me on the head with her long wooden spoon. "Good imagination," she said.

"Why don't you sit down at your computer and write up that story?" Dad added. "Maybe you're going to be a science fiction writer."

"*Aaaaaagh!*" I let out an angry cry. "It's *not* science fiction!" I screamed. "It's *real!*"

I could feel myself start to lose it. I almost

grabbed the spoon out of Mom's hand and tossed it out the window.

Almost. I caught myself just in time.

I balled my hands into tight fists at my sides and stomped out of the kitchen.

When those disgusting monsters and Mrs H and her commander ran the world, it wouldn't be so funny – *would* it?

I stormed into my room and slammed the door behind me.

I tossed my backpack on to the bed and started pacing furiously back and forth.

Who would believe me?

Would Daisy and DeWayne believe me? Maybe. But who cared? They couldn't help.

I needed to find somebody who could *stop* Mrs Hardesty.

Mr Wong? Maybe. The town police? Maybe. The military unit my cousin Brad is in? Maybe.

But they wouldn't believe me, either.

No one would believe me – unless I had *proof.*

I banged my forehead against the wall. I had my mobile phone with me in the attic. Why didn't I take pictures?

Why?

Now I knew what I had to do. I had to go back there and take good, clear pictures of those monsters. Then people would have to believe me.

I shuddered.

I had no choice. I was the only one in the world who knew about Mrs Hardesty's plot. I was the only one who could stop her.

I sat down at my computer. I messaged Daisy and DeWayne. I asked them to come with me, back to Mrs H's house. I told them it was a total emergency.

They both said no.

DeWayne wrote:

SOUNDS LIKE A BAD PLAN. NO WAY I'M EVER GOING ON HER STREET AGAIN.

Daisy wrote a very short message:

ALLERGIC TO GIANT EGGS. SORRY.

OK. OK. I was on my own.

"I can do this," I told myself. "They don't call me Monster for nothing."

Saturday morning, I checked out the camera in my mobile phone. I snapped some shots of Mom and Dad at breakfast, just to make sure it was working. Then I tucked it carefully into my jeans pocket.

Mom and Dad hurried off to play their Saturday morning golf game.

I hurried off to save the world.

Mrs Hardesty's blue car wasn't in her driveway. Was she away?

I circled the house a few times to make sure.

No signs of life. Nothing moving.

I crept up close to the front and peered into the living room window. I saw a newspaper folded up on the sofa. A coffee mug on the table beside it.

No Mrs Hardesty.

I crossed my fingers. Maybe she was out shopping for more meat or something. I could just slip down to the basement. Take a bunch of photos. And leave.

Maybe. . .

I crept around to the back. I peeked into the kitchen window.

"OH!"

I uttered a cry and dropped to the ground.

A green monster was standing in the kitchen – staring right out at me!

14

I hunched below the window, squeezing myself into a tight ball. And waited for the creature to stick its head out the window. Or to come flying out the back door to grab me.

But no.

After a minute or so, I realized it probably hadn't seen me. So I took a deep breath and pulled myself back up to the window.

The monster stood over the stove. It had a long white spatula tucked in one claw. It was stirring something in a big frying pan.

Eggs?

I squinted through the window. Yes, it was cooking up a big pan of eggs.

Now it had its back to me. I straightened up a little higher to see better.

How did it escape from the basement?

And how did it know how to cook?

A thousand questions whirred through my mind. I shook them away and reached into my jeans for my phone. I raised the phone to the window and steadied it.

No. No good. Too dark in the kitchen.

I clicked the phone shut and shoved it back into my jeans pocket. I pressed my nose against the window. I watched the monster stir the eggs with the long spatula.

And then the creature stuck out its other claw. It grabbed up a big hunk of egg and slid it into its mouth. It turned to the side. I could see the smile on its snout as it chewed.

It chewed the eggs for a short while, then swallowed.

And instantly, the monster began to change. Its whole shape wriggled and pulled in. Its green head shrunk and shifted – until it became a *human head*!

In seconds, the monster transformed into Mrs Hardesty!

I gasped. I nearly hit my head on the window.

Mrs Hardesty was a monster, too!

The eggs changed her back to her human body.

If only I had taken a picture.

If only Daisy and DeWayne had come with me. I'd have witnesses. I'd have proof.

I watched Mrs Hardesty reach into the pan. She picked up another chunk of scrambled egg. She took a big bite.

In seconds, she stood there – a monster again!

Another bite of egg. And she transformed back into Mrs Hardesty.

Wow! I couldn't believe what I was seeing. But I realized how powerful those eggs were. They could turn you from a monster into a human and back again – in seconds.

"No one will ever believe this!" I muttered to myself. And she planned to bring these eggs to school and feed them to everyone!

I slid down to the ground. I sat with my back to the wall, trying to think. Trying to make a plan.

How could I get pictures of this without being caught?

Even with the pictures, would anyone believe the power of the eggs?

I shook my head, trying to clear my brain.

And the back door swung open. Mrs Hardesty stepped out.

"Michael!" she cried. "I *thought* I saw you. What are you *doing* here?"

15

I struggled to my feet. "Uh . . . well. . ."

Panic froze my brain.

She stared at me, gripping the spatula tightly in one hand.

"Uh . . . I needed help," I said finally. "With a homework assignment. I . . . I thought maybe you could help me."

"On a Saturday morning?" she asked. "It's very early."

"You're right," I said. "What was I *thinking*?" I started to walk away.

"Come in, Michael," Mrs Hardesty said. "Don't hurry away. You're just in time. I want you to try my special eggs."

"Huh?" I gasped. *No way!*

I almost blurted out, "I saw what they do!" But I stopped myself at the last second.

"Come in, Michael." She held the door open.

"I can't," I said. "I'm late for . . . uh . . . I'm late for something."

Lame. How lame was that?

"It will only take a second," Mrs Hardesty said. "It's a new egg recipe. You'll be the first to try it."

No, I won't. I saw you try it!

"I . . . I think I might be allergic to eggs," I said.

She laughed. "Not these eggs. These eggs are special." Then her smile faded. "Michael, get in here," she ordered.

Before I knew it, I was sitting at her kitchen table.

Her dark eyes flashed as she set a big plate of eggs down in front of me. "I'm so glad you stopped by," she said.

I gulped – and gazed down at the eggs. They were fluffy and bright yellow. They didn't smell like eggs. They smelled kind of like hay and fertilizer. You know that smell when you drive past a farm in the summer?

"I can't," I said. "I'm sorry. I had such a huge breakfast." I started to stand up.

But Mrs Hardesty leaned over me, forcing me to sit back down. She took a fork and scooped a chunk of egg. Then she slid the fork into my mouth.

"Eat up, Michael," she said softly, her breath brushing my ear. "Delicious, right?"

I didn't want to swallow. But the egg

slid down my tongue. It tasted like chalk. Very dry.

My heart started to do a tap dance in my chest. My ears tingled.

Mrs Hardesty forced another forkful down my throat.

I was terrified and angry at the same time. She tried to feed me more. I shoved her hand away. The eggs went flying across the table.

Too late. Too late, I realized.

I already felt strange. My whole body tingled. My skin felt rubbery. I shuddered.

"You've been a lot of trouble, Michael," Mrs Hardesty said softly. She backed away. Her face was twisted in excitement.

"You've been a lot of trouble to me – haven't you?" she said. "But from now on, I think we're going to get along just fine!"

"Nooo—" I tried to cry out. But only a hoarse croak escaped my throat.

I felt my arms shrinking, my hands folding into my wrists. I raised them – and groaned. My skin was green and covered in bumps. In place of fingers, I had claws.

My stomach lurched. Strange sounds burst from my open mouth. I felt my face changing. I reached up and wrapped a claw around my long snout. A long, dry snake tongue whipped out of my mouth.

I leaped up from the kitchen table. I jumped right out of my clothes. My chair went flying backwards.

I tried to run – and tripped over my jeans. My lizardy body heaved in and out.

I'm a MONSTER! I realized. *It took only two little forkfuls – and I'm a MONSTER!*

I staggered back on my stubby legs. I felt sick. The room became a black-and-white blur. My tongue slid in and out.

Mrs Hardesty tossed back her head and laughed. "You look wonderful, Michael," she said. She slapped my green bumpy back.

"Unnnh unnnnnh." I couldn't make words.

"You're my little baby now," Mrs Hardesty said. "I'm going to keep you nice and safe with my other little babies. Won't that be fun?"

She dug her nails into my shoulders as she forced me down the basement stairs. Blocking my escape, she unlocked the door and pushed me in with the other monsters.

"See you later, little babies," she cooed. "Mama is going out to shop for supplies. I'm going to scramble up a big egg on Monday – big enough for the whole school!"

She laughed a cold laugh. "Who *said* teachers don't have fun!"

She slammed the door. I heard the click of the lock.

I spun away from the door and glanced around the room. Was there a window I could escape through? Another door?

I had to get out of there and warn everyone. She was planning to turn the whole school into monsters on Monday!

I shut my eyes, trying to think. Even if I escaped, how could I warn everyone? I couldn't even speak. Besides, who would listen to a lizardy green monster?

When I opened my eyes, I had a surprise. The other monsters had lined up. They stood in a straight line, staring at me.

Their tongues flicked in and out. They lowered their heads, opened their jaws, and uttered low growls.

Not friendly.

I didn't need any hints. I could see they weren't happy about me.

"Dudes, I'm on *your* side." That's what I wanted to say. Instead, it came out, *"Urrrrrf urrrrrrf."*

I started to back towards the door. But they moved quickly.

They slid across the floor and formed a circle around me.

I raised both front claws. *I surrender.*

It didn't impress them. The circle grew tighter as they closed in on me.

Closer . . . closer. . .

I was trapped in the middle. Nowhere to run.

Their growls grew louder. And what was that *snapping* sound?

Their jaws moving hungrily.

I gritted my teeth. I held my breath. And they pounced. . .

As they dived for me, I dropped to my stomach and hit the floor.

To my surprise, I heard the lock click on the other side of the door. And the door swung open.

The sudden movement made the monsters pull back.

Daisy and DeWayne poked their heads into the room.

"Michael? Are you in here?" Daisy called. "We've been looking everywhere—"

She stopped. They both let out horrified cries when they saw they had stepped into a roomful of *monsters*.

I was so happy to see them. My rescuers!

I stuck out my arms and went running to hug my friends.

A huge mistake.

They screamed again.

What would *you* do if you saw a six-foot-tall monster running at you?

DeWayne pulled back his arm – and gave me a hard punch under my snout.

"*UNNNNNH.*" The punch sent me flying back. Pain shot down my body. I dropped to my knees.

Daisy and DeWayne gaped down at me.

I waited for the room to stop spinning.

The other monsters were huffing and puffing again, hopping up and down excitedly.

"It's ME! Michael!" I shouted to Daisy and DeWayne. But it came out, "*Uuuunnngh urrrrf.*"

How could I make them understand?

How could I show them it was me?

I knew I had only a few seconds. My two horrified friends were already backing out of the room.

Once they closed the door, I'd be trapped. And no one would be able to stop Mrs Hardesty and her egg plot.

How could I let them know?

Something gleamed on the floor right outside the door. I squinted at it. Something silvery.

It took me a moment to realize it was my dog whistle.

So *that's* what fell from my pocket when we were down here with the black cat!

I stood up and moved slowly to it. With a quick swipe of my claw, I grabbed the whistle off the floor.

Please, I thought. *Please – let Daisy and DeWayne figure out that it's me!*

I sucked in a deep breath. Raised the dog whistle to my snout.

And started to blow.

Then I waved it in the air so they could see it. Then I blew it some more.

Please! Please...

17

I waved the whistle at them. Did they recognize it? I blew it some more.

Daisy and DeWayne had backed to the door. They stared at me, their faces scrunched up in confusion.

I blew another long blast.

To my shock, the monsters all started to whimper. They curled up on themselves, trying to cover their ears.

All of them were shaking and quaking.

Wow, I thought. *They definitely don't like high-pitched sounds.*

It hurt my ears, too. But I blew the whistle again.

The monsters hunched over, trembling, whimpering softly.

"Michael? Is that really *you*?" Daisy called.

"Are you nuts?" DeWayne snapped at her. "That's not Michael. That's a *monster* waving a dog whistle at us!"

"UNNNNH!" I cried. I raised the whistle to Daisy. I pointed it at myself.

Sign language. Desperate sign language.

"We're *out* of here!" DeWayne cried. "They're gonna eat us or something!"

But Daisy kept staring hard at me. "Michael?"

I nodded. I took a bow. I nodded some more. I waved the dog whistle in front of her.

"We've been looking *everywhere* for you!" Daisy cried. She realized it was me! "Did Mrs Hardesty do this to you?"

I nodded some more.

DeWayne was starting to believe, too. He pointed to the others. "Mrs Hardesty hatched all these from giant eggs?"

I nodded again.

I knew there wasn't time for any more questions. Mrs H would be back from the store at any minute.

I lowered my head and took off running. I burst between my two friends and out the door. My lizardy feet pounded the stairs up to the kitchen.

Daisy and DeWayne followed after me. No sign of Mrs Hardesty.

Now what?

I was free. Out of the basement room. But *no way* I could tell the whole story while I was still a monster.

My eyes darted around the kitchen. I saw my jeans and T-shirt piled in a corner. Then I gazed at the stove.

The eggs!

Were there any eggs left in the pan?

I pushed my two friends out of the way and stomped to the stove.

"Michael? What are you doing?" Daisy cried.

I looked down at the frying pan. Just a tiny chunk of egg left. A teaspoonful, stuck to the bottom.

Was it enough to turn me back into me?

It *had* to be!

I lowered my face into the pan. Flicked out my snaky tongue and wrapped it around the little piece of egg. I pulled it into my mouth and swallowed it.

Yes. Come on. Change, Michael! Change!

I waited. Waited. . .

Nothing happened.

18

No. Wait.

My stomach started to churn. The room tilted and swayed. My skin heated up. I felt as if my whole body was melting . . . melting to the floor.

I looked down. I still had claws. My lizard arms were green and bumpy.

But my legs were back. My feet. I stomped hard on the floor. Yes, my feet were there!

I hurried to the corner and pulled on my clothes. Then I trotted to the hall mirror – and gasped.

"Michael!" Daisy cried. "You're . . . back!"

"Kinda," DeWayne added.

I stared in the mirror.

My face . . . my head – they were back.

But my neck and chest were green. I still had monster arms and claws!

"Not enough eggs!" The words burst from my throat in a growl. "I need more eggs!"

I dived back to the stove. I scraped the bottom

of the pan with my claws. I pulled the pan off the stove and flipped it upside down.

No. None left.

I turned and saw my two friends staring at me in horror.

"Michael, how did this happen to you?" Daisy cried.

"No time to explain," I said. "Mrs Hardesty will be back any second."

"But . . . but you . . . you're still half monster!" DeWayne exclaimed.

I rolled my eyes. "Tell me something I don't know."

"But I don't understand," Daisy said, shaking her head. "Are you—"

"We'll talk later. We've got to get help – right away," I said. "Mrs Hardesty is a monster, too. She and her commander have a terrible plan. She's going to make a big batch of her eggs for the whole class. They . . . they plan to turn everyone in town into monsters!"

They both squinted at me. "Everyone in town?" DeWayne asked.

I headed to the back door. "Who can help us?" I asked. "Who?"

"How about Mr Wong?" Daisy said. "He lives down the street, remember?"

"Yeah," DeWayne said. "Wong said to come see him if we have a problem. And we *definitely* have a problem!"

"OK. It's a plan," I said. "Let's do it."

I grabbed the doorknob with one claw and pulled open the kitchen door. Bright sunlight greeted us as we ran out into the garden. I saw someone's big golden Lab sprawled on its back in the driveway. Squirrels darted for the trees when they saw us.

We ran to the back of the garden. The big skip was still in the plot. Someone had leaned a bike with no tyres against it.

We crossed the plot and made our way to Mr Wong's garden. My legs felt trembly and strange. I think they were still part monster legs.

Suddenly, I heard low grunts and growls behind us. And the thunder of heavy feet against the ground.

"Look!" DeWayne spun around and pointed. "Oh, no!"

I turned and saw the big green monsters lumbering after us. They moved in twos and threes, stumbling forward on their hind legs, eyes half shut in the bright sunlight.

Had they ever seen the sun before?

"We left the basement door open!" Daisy said. "They're following us."

The monsters began to growl. They bared their teeth as they lumbered after us. Some of them chewed up big clumps of earth and grass and spat them at us.

"We . . . can't outrun them," DeWayne murmured.

A wet clump of earth smacked me in the back. I shook it off.

"Not a problem!" I cried. "We're almost at Mr Wong's house. When Mr Wong sees them, he'll *have* to believe our story. He'll have to help us!"

Mr Wong had a small square house with red brick walls and white shutters on all the windows. A small satellite dish stood behind the garage. A vegetable garden stretched across the back. I almost stumbled over a rake half hidden by the tall grass as I ran around to the front.

He had a big screened porch facing the street. It was empty. I climbed the front step and rang the bell with one claw.

As we waited, the monsters lined up behind us in the grass. They snapped their jaws, preparing to attack. Thick drool ran down their jagged teeth. They pawed the ground impatiently.

Then they came at us a step at a time. Closer . . . closer. . .

I kept glancing behind me as I rang the bell again and again. The principal didn't answer.

"He's GOT to be home!" I boomed. "This is an emergency. Those monsters are HUNGRY!"

The monster part of me suddenly took over.

I lowered my big shoulder to the door – and

rammed it with my monster strength. The door cracked open. I led the way inside.

Mr Wong's living room was dark and silent. The curtains were pulled, and the lights were off. I saw a pile of school books on the coffee table.

I started to call his name, then stopped.

I saw a light in the next room. And heard voices.

I moved towards it. The room had a big flatscreen TV on the wall. An old black-and-white movie was on.

I stepped closer. I saw a dark sofa and a big armchair.

And then. . .

In the doorway to the TV room, I turned to my friends. "I don't think Mr Wong is going to be any help to us," I whispered.

Their faces filled with surprise. "Why not?" Daisy asked.

I moved back so they could see into the corner. And there sat Mr Wong – right on top of a giant egg.

He had his eyes closed. He didn't see us staring at him in shock from the doorway.

He had his suit jacket off. His tie was loosened. Perched on top of the egg, he leaned his back against the wall. His hands were clasped in his lap.

The egg was *twice* as big as the one in Mrs Hardesty's attic!

"Wow," DeWayne whispered, shaking his head. "He's hatching eggs, too. Do you believe it?"

"Let's get out of here," I whispered.

Daisy, DeWayne and I turned to leave. But our path was blocked.

The snarling monsters had followed us inside. Snapping their jaws, drooling, they pushed into the small living room. They knocked over tables and chairs and tore the carpet with their sharp claws.

As I stared in horror, they squeezed closer, forcing us back into the TV room.

"We're trapped," Daisy whispered. "We can't get out."

"They're going to CRUSH us!" DeWayne cried. "Crush us and then EAT us!"

I turned back to Mr Wong. How could he sleep through this?

"We have no choice. We have to run through the monsters," I said. "No other way out."

But before we could move, I heard the front door slam. A few seconds later, Mrs Hardesty stepped into the room. She carried a platter heaped high with scrambled eggs.

Mrs H had a big smile on her face as she entered. But it faded instantly when she saw the roomful of monsters.

Her mouth dropped open in an O of shock. And she nearly dropped the egg platter.

The monsters forgot about us and turned to greet her. Daisy, DeWayne and I scrunched down and hid behind the monsters. They began jumping up and down with excitement and making shrill crying noises.

But she wasn't happy to see them. "How did you escape?" she cried. "Who let you out?"

And then she shouted to the sleeping principal: "Commander Xannx! WAKE UP!"

Behind us, on top of his egg, Mr Wong blinked a few times.

"Commander – what is *happening* here?" Mrs Hardesty shouted. "My babies! My babies have escaped!"

Daisy, DeWayne and I exchanged glances. So Mr Wong was Commander Xannx!

"My babies! My babies!" Mrs Hardesty cried. "How did you get over here?"

Daisy, DeWayne and I tried to scrunch down even more. But it didn't take long for Mrs Hardesty to spot us.

Her pale face darkened. Her eyes narrowed. "YOU!" she screamed. "YOU evil kids let them out!"

Behind us, Mr Wong shook himself awake. "What is happening here?" he called. "Hyborg? Is that you?"

Balancing the egg platter in one hand, Mrs Hardesty pointed to her monsters. "Attack those kids!" she ordered them in a deep growl.

My heart skipped a beat. I glanced around quickly. How to escape?

Mr Wong behind us. Mrs Hardesty and the monsters in front of us.

It didn't look good.

"Attack those kids!" Mrs Hardesty screamed. "Protect the Commander! I ORDER you to attack!"

The monsters tossed back their heads and roared. The noise shook the room.

I felt weak. Trapped. Nowhere to move.

Snapping their jaws, rolling their eyes wildly, they came for us.

20

I felt something explode in my chest. Was it fear? Was it anger?

I didn't have time to think about it. I only knew that I wasn't going to stand there and let Mrs Hardesty's monsters attack us.

I was still only half human. And as the monsters lumbered forward, I let the beast in me take over.

"They call me MONSTER!" I cried. "And I *am* a monster!"

With an animal cry, I spun around. And slammed my claws into the giant eggshell.

Mr Wong uttered a startled shout. His arms flew up as the eggshell cracked.

The crack was loud enough to silence the monsters. I saw the jagged line spread down the egg from top to bottom.

And then, with another loud *CRAAAAACK*, the top of the shell fell in.

Mr Wong uttered a cry. His hands shot straight up in the air – and *he dropped into the egg*!

He made a loud splash. He kicked out a small jagged piece of shell. I could see him thrashing and kicking under the thick yellow yolk.

His head sank under the yolky yellow slime, then slid up again. He was sputtering and choking. He sank again. Then pushed his face above the thick surface.

"I can't swim!" he screamed. "Get me out of here! I can't swim! Hyborg-Xrxuz – help me!"

"Coming, Commander!" she cried. She dived towards the egg.

But the monster anger still burned in my chest. I lifted Mrs Hardesty – or whatever her name was – off the floor with my claws.

She squirmed and struggled. But I was too strong for her.

I held her high – and *heaved* her over the top into the giant egg.

She made a big splash. She and Wong struggled, climbing over each other, twisting and kicking. Sputtering, they sank beneath the yellow yolk.

Their mouths opened to scream. They swallowed egg yolk.

As my friends and I stared in amazement, they both began to change. Their skin turned green. Their human faces shifted into green monster heads. Their bodies ballooned and twisted.

And now we were watching two green monsters. Slapping their claws at each other, wrestling, snarling like beasts, they floundered and thrashed inside the egg.

In seconds, they pulled each other down ... down to the bottom of the egg.

I couldn't see them through the thick yellow goo.

Daisy, DeWayne and I stood gaping at the egg. Watching for them. . . Watching. . .

They didn't come back up.

Whew.

I breathed a sigh of relief. The evil aliens had been defeated – thanks to me, Monster Munroe.

Daisy and DeWayne flashed me the thumbs up sign.

But we had no time to celebrate.

The other monsters remained silent for a few seconds more. They stared at the egg as if waiting for their two leaders to return.

And then they opened their mouths in one long angry roar. Their eyes turned red with fury. They raised their heads and snapped their jaws hungrily. And came at us, their feet thudding on the carpet.

I swallowed hard, watching them attack. And thought: *I can't fight them all – CAN I??*

I planted my feet and raised my claws in front of me. I gritted my teeth and prepared for a battle.

No need.

The attacking monsters had no interest in my friends and me.

They dived head first at the platter of eggs on the floor. Snarling, slapping each other away, fighting, slurping loudly, they gobbled up the eggs.

Daisy, DeWayne and I didn't move. I kept my claws raised. I held my breath.

I watched the monsters devour the eggs. Seconds later, their bodies began to change. Their green skin faded to a lighter shade. They turned yellow, and their skin began to bubble.

"They – they're turning to *liquid*!" DeWayne cried.

Yes. He was right. Their bones shrank. Their

heads melted away. Their bodies plopped wetly to the floor.

In seconds, they had become yellow puddles on the carpet.

I knew what was happening. "The eggs – they turn you back to what you were originally," I said. "So . . . the monsters turned back into *egg yolks*!"

"We won! We beat them!" Daisy cried, pumping her fists in the air.

I tried to slap her a high five. Then I remembered I still had monster claws.

"One more thing to do," I said. I lowered my face to the giant cracked egg. And I licked some yolk off the shell.

Yuck. It tasted totally gross. Lumpy like sour milk. I almost puked. But I choked it down.

Then I stared at my claws . . . and waited.

Yesssss!

A few seconds later, my arms stretched out. My hands returned. My skin turned back to its original colour.

"I'm a *human* again!" I shouted, jumping up and down. "I'm totally human! I don't want anyone to ever call me *Monster* again!"

Stepping over the puddles of egg yolk, we started towards the door.

"Can you believe it?" Daisy said. "We just saved the world from evil aliens."

"No one will ever believe it," I said.

DeWayne stopped me at the door. "Yes, they will," he said. "I've got proof."

He held up his mobile phone and grinned. "I've been snapping photos the whole time. I've got Mrs Hardesty, the monsters, Mr Wong – everything. Got it all right here."

"You do?" I cried. I gave him a hard slap on the back. "That's awesome. Let me see."

I took the phone from him and flipped it open. I scrolled through his snapshots. All feet. Just shoes. DeWayne's shoes. Picture after picture.

I handed the phone back to him. "DeWayne, did you ever take pictures before with this phone?" I asked.

"No. It's a new phone."

He glanced through the snapshots. Then he shook his head sadly. "Guess we *don't* have proof. . ."

"Michael, I've never seen you eat like that!" Mom exclaimed at dinner. "Be careful. Don't eat the place mat!"

Dad laughed. "Guess you worked up an appetite, huh?" he said. "Did you have a busy day?"

"Yeah. Kind of busy," I said.

Of course, I didn't tell them about Commander Xannx or Hyborg-Xrxuz. Or their monsters. Or saving the whole planet from evil aliens.

I had no proof.

"What's for dessert?" I asked.

Mom sliced large pieces of cake for the three of us. I grabbed my fork and started to shovel it into my mouth.

I'd never been so starving in my life. And this cake tasted awesome! The three of us ate in silence for a while.

"Isn't it good?" Mom said. "Mrs Hardesty brought it over yesterday."

"Huh?" I tried to talk, but I had a mouthful of cake.

"Wasn't that nice of her to bring us dessert?" Mom said. "She said she made it with her own special eggs!"

ENTER
HORRORLAND

THE STORY SO FAR...

Several kids received mysterious invitations to be Very Special Guests at HorrorLand theme park. They looked forward to a week of scary fun. But the scares quickly became **TOO REAL** when Slappy the evil dummy, Dr Maniac and other menacing villains started to appear.

Two Very Special Guests—Britney Crosby and Molly Molloy—disappeared in a café with a mirrored wall. The others have been trying desperately to find them. The park guides—called *Horrors*—have been no help at all.

Except for one Horror, called Byron. He warned the kids they were all in danger. He said he'd help them escape from HorrorLand. He gave them tokens, which turned out to be tracking devices.

Was he trying to protect them? Most of the kids didn't like the idea of being spied on. They gave away their tokens.

Byron told them to meet him at the Bat Barn and he'd explain what was going on. But he didn't show up – and the kids were attacked by bats. The Bat Barn was supposed to be a fun attraction. But these bats were REAL!

Michael Munroe arrived the day before. And now he finds himself in a terrifying battle in the Bat Barn with the other Very Special Guests. He continues the story. . .

1

Red-eyed bats shrieked as they darted and swooped over us. I ducked as a bat whistled past my head, then soared up to the rafters of the barn.

Kids screamed and covered their faces. I swung both arms hard and swatted a bat off a girl's shoulder.

"The bats are REAL!" someone screamed.

"It's supposed to be a JOKE!" a boy cried.

A fat creature thudded into my chest, wings flapping furiously. Sharp claws dug into my T-shirt. I gripped the bat with both hands and flung it off me.

My new friend, Abby Martin, pressed her hands over her face. She screamed as a bat danced on her head, pulling at her hair. With a loud cry, I slapped it away.

My second day as a Very Special Guest at HorrorLand. It wasn't exactly what I had imagined.

Where was that Horror, Byron? The tall one with the yellow horns? He told us to meet him here.

We didn't have time to think about him. The screeching, glowing-eyed bats were out for blood.

The barn was big and dark. The doors had closed behind us. The only light came from a narrow window high in the roof of the barn.

In the darkness, it seemed like a *thousand* wings were beating around us. A *thousand* shrill creatures zooming low, tearing and biting at us.

Abby screamed again. I lurched towards her and stumbled over a pile of straw. Suddenly, I had an idea. Could I stop the bat attack?

The kids back home call me Monster. Believe me, I know a *lot* about monsters – because I WAS one! My parents and I would still be monsters. But I led them to Mr Wong's house. Talk about luck! There was enough of the disgusting egg yolk left to turn us back to humans.

It's a long story. But ever since, I always carry my lucky dog whistle with me. I pulled it out of my jeans pocket and raised it to my mouth.

Would it be lucky *now*?

Yes! Seconds later, the shrill bat cries stopped. A strange hush fell over the barn.

The bats appeared to freeze in mid-air. They stopped their furious flapping. They glided up to the rafters.

They didn't come back down.

The other kids were blinking, shaking and shivering, gazing around in confusion. Carly Beth and Sabrina dropped to their knees in the straw. Robby spun around in a circle, hands raised. The bats were gone, but he was still fighting them off.

"Hey, Michael—" Matt strode up to me. "How did you do that? How did you stop the bats?"

I raised my dog whistle. "Had this in my jeans," I said. "Thought I'd give it a try. I guess the sound hurt them or confused them or something."

"Good work, Michael," Abby said. Her hands trembled as she tugged at her long black hair, trying to smooth it down. She slapped me a high five. "That was scary."

Billy Deep and his sister, Sheena, stared at the rafters. "They're still up there," Sheena murmured. "Think they'll attack again?"

"We're outta here," Matt said. He pushed past me and led the way to the barn doors. He shoved one open.

Late afternoon sunlight poured in. We followed him to a small grassy field beside the barn.

Sabrina gazed around. "Where is Byron?" she asked. "He was supposed to meet us here."

"Must've got held up," Robby said.

"What if it was an ambush?" I said. I tapped the dog whistle against my palm. My skin still tingled from the touch of the bat claws.

"What if this dude Byron planned the whole thing?" I asked.

"You mean he told us to come here knowing the bats would attack?" Abby asked.

"No way!" Matt replied, shaking his head. "Byron is our only friend here."

"Matt's right," Billy said. "He's the only Horror who told us the truth. Byron warned us we were all invited here for a reason. He told us we were all in danger."

"But Byron is the one who gave us those tokens, right?" I said. "And they turned out to be tracking devices. He wanted to spy on us."

I pointed to the Bat Barn. "And now he sent us here to be *creamed* by screaming bats!"

"Don't accuse Byron," Matt said, narrowing his eyes at me.

I started to lose it. "Sorry if Byron is your *hero* – but I'll accuse whoever I want!" I snapped.

Matt clenched his hands into fists. He was a big dude, almost as big as me. "You just got here, Michael," he said, sneering. "You don't know enough to start mouthing off."

I should've just shut up. But that would be a first.

"I know enough to fight back when I'm in trouble," I said. "I don't just stand around like you – shaking like a wimp, waiting for someone to come help me!"

"Stop it, you two!" Sabrina cried. "We don't have time—"

Too late.

Matt rushed at me. I timed it just right – and gave him a hard *BUMP* with my chest.

His eyes went wide with surprise. He stumbled back. And landed on his bum in a wide patch of mud.

With a furious cry, he leaped to his feet. Grabbed me by the shoulders. Pulled me down into the mud. And we started wrestling.

"Stop it! Stop it!" Sabrina grabbed my shoulders and tried to pull me off Matt. But she wasn't strong enough.

I grabbed Matt's head and pushed his face into the mud.

He came up sputtering.

"What are you fighting for?" Abby cried. "We're in danger! We have to stay on the same side!"

Matt spat a mouthful of mud in my face. I pushed his shoulders down and pinned him to the ground.

"Stop! Stop the fight!"

I heard two voices I didn't recognize.

I raised my head. Turned – and saw two black-and-orange-uniformed Monster Police running towards us, swinging wooden clubs.

"Dudes – RUN!" Billy screamed.

I jumped to my feet and helped pull Matt up from the mud.

Why were we fighting? I couldn't remember.

As they stampeded towards us, the Monster Police waved their sticks and screamed at us to stop. I knew they wouldn't hurt us. I mean, we were guests at the park – right?

But I took off anyway. We all did. We ran in different directions.

I was close behind Abby for a while. But then I lost her in the crowd. And then I lost *myself* in the crowd!

Where was I? I was running full speed now along a wire fence. On the other side, I saw kids on a beach. The kids were screaming and laughing, sinking into the sand.

Finally, I saw a sign: QUICKSAND BEACH. DROP IN ANY TIME!

It looked like fun. I spun around. I'd lost the two Monster Policemen.

I took a few minutes to catch my breath. Then I made my way back to Stagger Inn.

A short while later, everyone gathered in my room on the thirteenth floor. Matt and I stared at each other with our hands in our jeans pockets. Then we both apologized at once. We even shook hands.

"We're cool?" I asked.

"We're cool," Matt said.

"Look, we're all scared and stressed out," Carly Beth said. "But we have to stick together."

She sighed and dropped down on to the edge of my bed next to her friend Sabrina. "Sabrina and I didn't believe any of this," she said. "You know. About the missing girls and the other park."

"But we do now," Sabrina said.

"Look, Abby and I just got here yesterday," I said. "We don't know why everyone is so nervous. Tell us what's up."

They all started talking at once. Finally, Matt said he'd try to explain everything.

"As soon as I arrive," he started, "this Horror called Byron runs up to me. He says I'm in danger. And he gives me this."

Matt pulled a grey plastic card from his wallet. "It's a room key card," he said. "But it's not from HorrorLand. And it seems to have special powers. It helped me win at the carnival games. And it opens doors that regular key cards don't open—"

"Our first day, my sister Sheena and I met these two girls," Billy Deep interrupted. "Molly Molloy and Britney Crosby. Then they disappeared. Gone. *Poof.* We've been searching for them ever since."

"The Horrors won't help us," Sheena said. "They say the girls were never here."

"We saw them in a café with a big mirrored wall," Matt said. "This key card opened the door to the café. But when we went inside, the girls were gone."

"The mirror was soft, like liquid," Sheena explained. "I stuck my arm into it – and I disappeared, too. It's all very hazy. But I think I ended up in a different park."

"Byron keeps leaving us hints about another park," Matt said. He held up the two pieces of an old park guide. One showed a carousel with flames shooting out of it. It was called The Wheel of Fire. The other showed a hall of mirrors, called Mirror Mansion.

"Strange characters keep following us here," Robby said. "Trying to frighten us. We've all had scary problems back home. And they've followed us to the park!"

"When we looked into a piece of mirror, we

saw Britney and Molly on that burning carousel," Billy said.

"I think we're in real danger," Carly Beth said. "We need to make a plan. We need to get out of this park."

"Whoa. Wait a sec," I said. "Tell me more about the mirrors. All this stuff about mirrors is really interesting."

"I searched my whole room," Abby said. "I couldn't find a mirror anywhere. Whoever heard of a hotel room without mirrors?"

Again, everyone started talking at once. None of us had mirrors in our rooms.

"This is totally disturbing," I said. "It means we have to find a mirror. Mirrors must be a very important clue."

"We have to find Byron first," Matt said. "He's the only one who can tell us what's going on."

I didn't want to fight with Matt again. I could see he wanted to be leader of the group. And that was OK with me.

But once I get something in my head, I can't get it out. And right then, mirrors were definitely in my head.

So we split up. They all went out to search for Byron. And I went on a hunt for a mirror. We planned to meet in Matt's room in two hours.

I searched every inch of my room first. The

other kids were right. No mirror. Nothing even shiny enough to be used as a mirror.

I was dying to know why.

What if I just ask someone for a mirror? I thought.

It seemed like a good plan. I took the dark, creaky lift down to the hotel lobby. The lift had thick cobwebs hanging from its roof. Eerie organ music played all the way down.

But I wasn't in the mood for that kind of scary fun. I was on a mission.

I stepped up to the front desk. A green-skinned Horror with curly green hair and one brown eye and one blue eye stood behind the counter. He wore a bright purple tuxedo and lacy white shirt. A very colourful dude.

His name tag read: BOOMER. He looked up from his laptop. "Help you?"

"Yes," I said. "Do you have a mirror I could borrow?"

"A mirror?" he replied, squinting at me with his brown eye.

"Yes, do you have a mirror?" I repeated.

He smiled. "Sure thing," he said. "No problem."

I blinked. *That was easy.*

Then Boomer's smile grew wider. He leaned closer over the counter. "With *your* face, sonny, are you *sure* you want a mirror?" He burst out laughing.

Ha-ha.

I didn't crack a smile. "Yes," I said. "I couldn't find a mirror in my room."

"Of course not," he said.

"I don't get it," I said. "Why aren't there any mirrors here?"

Boomer lowered his voice to a whisper. "Because a lot of our guests are vampires," he said. "It makes them sad to pass a mirror and not see their reflection. We're just trying to be considerate, see?"

I felt myself start to get steamed. "Boomer," I said, "I'm not going to get a straight answer from you – am I?"

He shook his head. "No, you're not," he replied.

"Well . . . can you tell me where I might find a mirror?" I asked.

He thought for a moment. "Have you tried Mirror Lake?"

"Excuse me?" I said. "Mirror Lake? Is that in this park?"

He shrugged. "I don't know. I just made it up." He laughed again.

Ha-ha. The dude was a riot.

"Thanks a bunch," I said. I turned and walked out of the hotel. I knew I'd find a mirror *somewhere* in HorrorLand.

I tried the shops first. Clothing stores always have mirrors. I walked into a shop called FUR GET IT. They had T-shirts and caps "made of genuine werewolf fur".

I tried on a cap. It was way itchy. I asked the sales clerk behind the counter for a mirror so I could see how the cap looked.

"Sorry, kid," he said. "No mirrors here. We're very superstitious. What if we broke one? Seven years' bad luck."

That made me think of Mrs Hardesty – or whatever her real name was. She was superstitious, too.

I tried the mask store across the road. No mirrors.

I tried three more shops. No mirrors anywhere.

This was definitely a mystery that needed to be solved.

I began stopping people who passed by. "Do you have a mirror I could borrow? It's really important."

Most of them thought I was crazy. Or they thought it was some kind of HorrorLand joke. They just kept walking.

I was ready to give up. The sun was sinking behind the trees of Wolfsbane Forest. I felt tired and hungry. And angry that I couldn't find such a simple thing as a mirror.

I guess my nickname – Monster – is a good one. When things don't go my way, I can feel my anger start to boil up.

I turned back towards the hotel. My brain was spinning with the story of the two girls who disappeared in the café with the soft, liquid mirror.

Then a small black-and-white sign caught my eye. It was on the wall of a low white building, set back from the street. The building had a narrow white door and no windows.

The sign read: OFF-LIMITS. STAFF ONLY. DO NOT ENTER.

I read the sign three times. Then I stepped up to the narrow door. Was the door locked?

Normally, I would have obeyed the sign. But right now I was feeling angry and frustrated. I don't like mysteries. I wanted to solve this one quickly.

I turned the knob. The door opened easily. Did someone forget to lock it?

I stepped inside and closed it behind me. I was in a tiny square hallway. In front of me – a concrete stairway leading steeply down.

A sign above the stairway read: DO NOT ENTER.

I peered down the stairs. Too dark to see anything down there. Silence. No sounds floating up.

Maybe they hide all the mirrors here, I told myself. *Maybe I'll find stacks and stacks of mirrors.*

I knew that was dumb. But I had to find out what was down there. I took a deep breath and started down the stairs.

My shoes thudded on the concrete. The stairs seemed to go down for ever.

I stopped halfway and squinted into the dim light. I still couldn't see anything. Just a high concrete wall.

No people. No Horrors. No sounds.

I climbed the rest of the way down. Gazing all around, I found myself in an enormous cavern. It seemed to stretch for *miles*!

It was silent there. I could hear my footsteps echo off the concrete walls.

I came to a dark tunnel entrance in the wall.

Glancing around, I saw dozens of tunnels heading off in all directions.

Fat pipes and electrical cables stretched down the tunnels. From deep in the tunnel, I could hear the hum of machinery.

I jumped when I heard a shrill *BEEP BEEP BEEP*.

Spinning around, I saw a row of robots shuffling out of one tunnel. Dozens of them. They looked like shiny metal wheelbarrows with heads and arms. A wheel in front and two short legs at the back.

Their heads were round and covered in control buttons and dials. The heads were spinning and *beeping* as the wheelbarrow bodies rolled across the floor. Each wheelbarrow carried a large wooden crate.

I stood frozen, watching them. Finally, they disappeared into another tunnel.

Alone again, I moved to the next tunnel. I could see two rows of computer screens and keyboards all down the tunnel.

The controls are here underground, I realized. *Everything that runs the park. The tunnels must stretch from one end of HorrorLand to the other.*

It's all electronic. Computerized. No people, I realized.

Wrong!

I gasped as a powerful hand grabbed me tightly by the shoulder and spun me around.

My mouth dropped open but no sound came out.

I stared up at a giant Horror. He must have been at least eight feet tall!

He had long black horns standing straight up from the thick brown fur of his head. He wore a black-and-orange Monster Police uniform, tight over his massive chest.

He gripped my shoulders and didn't let go. And stared down at me with cold black eyes.

"Kid," he boomed. *"You've made a bad mistake."*

I don't scare easy. After all, I faced *real* monsters back home, and I defeated them all.

But this dude was a GIANT!

"I – I know I made a mistake," I stammered. *Think fast, Michael.*

"I . . . thought . . . this was the Doom Slide," I said. "Some kids pointed me here. They said this was the Doom Slide ride."

He didn't let go of my shoulders. He leaned over me. His breath smelled of onions. "Kid, can you read?" he asked.

I nodded. "Yeah. Oh. You mean those signs?"

"Right. The *Do Not Enter* signs," he said. "You read them?"

"I thought they were a joke," I said. "You know. Part of the Doom Slide. Like, to scare kids. Like everything else here."

His deep black eyes burned into mine. He was trying to decide if he should believe me or not.

"You could get lost down here," he said in a low whisper. "You could get lost in these tunnels *for ever.*"

A chill tightened the back of my neck. Was he *threatening* me?

He let go of my shoulders. He stepped back. His shadow on the floor stretched for miles. "The signs were real," he said. "Go back outside, kid. Walk straight to Zombie Plaza. Then follow the signs to the Doom Slide."

"OK. Thanks," I said. I turned and hurried to the stairs.

"Sorry if I scared you," he called after me.

Was he kidding? I didn't wait to find out.

We met in Matt's room a short while later. The other kids had no luck, either. No sign of the Horror called Byron.

We were all hot and tired and jittery. We weren't having any fun. And we weren't getting anywhere.

What was going on in this creepy park? We still didn't have a clue.

But we couldn't stop discussing it.

"I had that golden token," Robby said. "It said *Panic Park* – remember?"

"In the vampire restaurant, I stared into the token," Abby said. "And I started to feel strange. Like it was pulling me. Pulling me into it."

"Abby, could you see your reflection in it?" I asked. "Was it like a mirror?"

Abby nodded yes.

"What happened to it?" I asked.

"A waitress took it," Robby said. "She thought it was her tip."

"OK. But this is cool!" I said, suddenly excited. "A coin can act like a mirror, right?"

"It has to be real shiny," Robby said.

"Come on," I said. "Who has a shiny coin? Get 'em out."

We all searched our pockets. I pulled out five or six coins from my jeans. They were all rubbed dull. No shiny ones.

Angrily, I tossed them on to the floor. "Anyone?" I cried.

No. We had only old scuffed coins.

Lots of groans of disappointment.

"Don't give up," Matt said. "We can't give up. We're really in danger here. And Byron is gone. There's no one to help us."

"I'll be right back," I said. I hurried to my room and grabbed my laptop. I carried it back to Matt's room.

"Let's search the Internet for the words *Panic Park*," I said. "Let's find out everything we can about it."

I started to boot up the computer.

"You can't," Matt said. "There's no Internet."

"Our mobile phones don't work, either," Billy said.

"There's no way to get online," Sheena said. "I guess they don't use computers here."

"Are you *joking*?" I cried. "The whole place is run by computers! I've *seen* them!"

I tapped away, but I couldn't get online. No wireless connection. No connection of any kind.

But it didn't matter. I suddenly knew what we had to do. I had a plan.

A dangerous plan.

"Follow me," I said.

I led them to the white building with the DO NOT ENTER sign.

It was a warm, sunny day. The park was jammed with people.

We passed long lines of kids waiting to get into the Werewolf Petting Zoo and the Haunted Theatre. People were even crowding around the cart that sold larvae-flavoured ice cream.

We passed several Horrors. But they didn't pay any attention to us.

I stopped at the front door of the building. "It's all underground," I explained. "Lots of tunnels going everywhere. We can hide down there. Then I can finally get online. No problem."

Carly Beth and Sabrina glanced around nervously. "Are you sure about this?" Sabrina asked. "Those warning signs look serious."

"No big deal," I said. "We're special guests. If we get caught, they'll just send us back to our rooms. Right?"

A few kids muttered, "Right." The others weren't so sure.

I grabbed the knob and tried to pull the door open.

Locked.

I tugged harder.

No way. This time, someone had remembered to lock it.

"That was a long walk for nothing," Billy grumbled.

Matt shoved me out of the way. "Let's try this," he said. He raised his strange key card to the door – and it swung open!

We touched knuckles. "Hey, I'm impressed," I said.

"It's all in the wrist," Matt said. He tucked the card back into his wallet.

That was the last joke anyone made. Everyone turned very serious as we made our way down the steep steps and into the huge concrete cavern.

The air grew warmer, heavy and damp. In the far distance, I could hear the roar of machinery and the *beep beep* of the wheelbarrow robots carrying their packages. The sounds echoed in the vast cavern.

I stopped at the bottom of the stairs and glanced around. No guards. No sign of that eight-foot-tall dude.

"Follow me," I whispered. We kept close to the

wall and edged our way to the first tunnel. I squinted into the dim light. The tunnel was jammed with old signs and stage props and furniture.

"Is that guillotine real?" Billy asked, pointing.

"Hope not," I said. "But we can hide behind it."

I led them into the tunnel. We hunched down behind the guillotine. I kept peering around. Tense. Expecting a guard to come jumping out at us.

I sat on the floor with my back against the tunnel wall. I propped my laptop on my lap and started typing. "Yesss!" I cried. "I knew it. There's a wireless connection down here."

Carly Beth leaned over my shoulder. "Type in *HorrorLand*," she said. "We've got to find out what's going on here."

A few seconds later, I found a long article about HorrorLand. I started reading it to the others.

"'HorrorLand theme park was built in the mid-1970s. It was the brainchild of a man named Kit Katzman. Katzman was a huge horror fan his entire life.

"'He populated the park with strange-looking workers named *Horrors*. At first, Katzman thought they were wearing costumes and masks. Later, he wasn't so sure.'"

Matt grabbed my shoulder. "This stuff isn't helping us," he said. "Look up *Panic Park*. See what it says."

I did a search for *Panic Park*. I clicked on several links. But for some reason, they had been deleted or shut down. Finally, I found an article titled "Vanished Amusement Parks."

I started to read it to everyone.

"'Panic Park was built in the 1950s by an odd, private man named Karloff Mennis. It was a park designed for people who liked the worlds of horror, fantasy and the bizarre.'"

Matt shook his head. "Scroll down," he said. "We don't care about the 1950s. What about *today*?"

"Wait! Wait!" I cried. "This is good. Listen to this. It's about that carousel ride. The one that's on fire."

I read from my laptop screen. "'The Wheel of Fire was one of the most popular rides at Panic Park. People loved twirling around while their horses flamed.'"

"So . . . that page Byron left us," Sheena said. "It was definitely from Panic Park."

"Byron was leaving us clues about Panic Park," Matt said. "He must want us to find out more about it."

"We . . . we saw Britney and Molly on that ride," Billy said.

Robby stared at the screen. "And that golden token I had – it came from Panic Park," he said.

"Let's see what else we can find out about Panic Park," I said. I leaned close to the screen and clicked on a few more links.

"Wait. Check this out," I said. "It's a blog. By a boy and a girl. Luke and Lizzy somebody. They say they spent some time in HorrorLand. But – whoa. I don't *believe* this. They are warning us. In their blog. They—"

My voice was drowned out by a high, shrill siren. So loud I pressed my hands over my ears.

And then we heard a voice booming through the sound system: "INTRUDERS! INTRUDERS! LOCKDOWN! INTRUDERS!"

We jumped to our feet. A chill shot down my back. I could hear shouts. Heavy, running footsteps in all directions.

"How did they find us?" Matt whispered.

"I know," Carly Beth said. "Sabrina and I made a terrible mistake. We never should have kept the tracking tokens Byron gave us."

The two girls tossed their tokens far into the tunnel.

"They're hiding in Tunnel B-4!" a deep voice boomed. The alarm siren rose and fell. The thundering footsteps grew louder.

"Let's go!" I cried.

We ran deeper into the tunnel. Was there a way to escape? We didn't know.

We ran from the footsteps and the loud, angry voices. The tunnel twisted and turned. The light grew dimmer. We ducked beneath cables and wires and tangles of cords.

"Tunnel B-4!" the loudspeaker echoed behind us. "Intruders! Tunnel B-4!"

Breathing hard, we stopped at a narrow door. It had the word LAB painted on the front.

Matt raised his key card to the door, and it swung open. "Maybe we can hide in here," he said.

He and I led the way in. The room was long and narrow. Lit by a row of dim fluorescent lights on the ceiling.

I waited for my eyes to adjust. Then I saw a long row of lab tables. Behind them, tall cabinets lined the wall.

"Are those cages?" Carly Beth pointed to the big boxes in the centre of the room.

We took a few steps towards them – then stopped.

"Oh, wow!"

"I don't believe this!"

"Are they real?"

We all gasped in shock – and stared at the ugly creatures inside the barred cages. They were dark and furry, like gorillas. Except their faces . . . their faces were almost human.

They had bald heads with long pointed ears. And they all had bright blue eyes. Human eyes.

But their fat bodies were covered with black fur. And they had big paws with curled claws, like bears.

They gnashed their teeth. Drool spilled from their mouths. They stuck their long furry arms out through the bars and swiped at us.

"Gorilla creatures!" Sheena cried. "Are they real? Are they robots or something?"

They sure looked real. "Maybe they are some kind of lab experiments," I said.

The ugly creatures grunted and gnashed their teeth. They pushed against the bars of their cages, trying to get at us.

"We can't stay here," I said. "We have to—"

The door burst open. Ten or twelve Monster Police came running in. Shouting, they waved wooden clubs above their heads.

"Freeze!" one of them boomed. "If you move, you'll be gorilla food!"

I glanced around. No other door. No way to escape.

The Monster Police formed a tight line. No way we could make a mad dash for the door.

They backed us up against the cages. The gorilla creatures swiped the air, trying frantically to grab us. They roared and slammed their cages.

My mind spun. I had an idea. I turned to Matt. "Quick – hand me that key card."

He started to reach into his jeans pocket. "What are you going to do with it, Michael?" he whispered.

"Try to open some cages," I said. "Let a few monsters out. You know. Distract the MPs. While they're chasing the gorillas, maybe we can get away."

Matt blew a long breath through his lips. We both knew it was a crazy idea.

But sometimes crazy ideas are the best ideas.

He pulled the key card from his pocket. I grabbed for it.

"NOOO!" I yelled as it fell out of my hand. I watched in horror as the card hit the floor – and slid under one of the cages.

We're doomed! I thought.

But Matt dived to the cage and dropped to his knees. He bent down low and slid one hand under the bottom of the cage.

And then we all cried out as one of the gorilla creatures reached out of the cage. It grabbed Matt with both paws – and lifted him off the floor!

Matt let out a scream. The gorilla creature pulled him up – then *crushed* him against the cage bars. It was trying to *pull* him into its cage!

Matt thrashed his arms and legs. But the beast had a powerful grip. Matt couldn't break free. He screamed again as the gorilla slammed him against the bars.

I dived to the ground. Reached under the cage. Slid my fingers around the key card. Then I raised it and waved it in front of the lock.

Would it work?

Yes! The cage door swung open.

It took the creature a few seconds to realize the door was open. Then it dropped Matt to the floor and came lumbering out of the cage on two legs.

"STOP RIGHT THERE!" an MP boomed. "WHAT ARE YOU DOING? ARE YOU CRAZY?"

Matt looked dazed. But he scrambled back to the other kids while I dived for the next cage. I held up the key card. The cage door swung open, and another gorilla beast eagerly staggered out.

The two creatures stared at each other. They both growled.

I let out a third gorilla. It stumbled out of its cage, drooling and rolling its blue human eyes.

The MPs were screaming at us, waving their clubs.

The three creatures stood between the cages, eyeing each other. And then with a deafening roar, they leaped at each other.

As I watched in amazement, they began to wrestle. They pounded each other with their big paws. Scratched at each other's faces. Rolled on the floor, snarling and groaning.

The MPs rushed to break up the fight.

That left the door unguarded.

In seconds, we all tore through it. Back into the tunnel. We turned and ran. No MPs out there. We could hear the monstrous fight grow louder in the lab behind us.

We ran deeper into the tunnel. We didn't talk. We didn't stop running.

Above us, we saw signs . . . DOOM SLIDE . . . A-NILE-ATOR . . . QUICKSAND BEACH. . .

We were running underneath those attractions. At each sign, a ladder led up to the top of the tunnel.

I stopped at a sign that read: GOODBYE LAND.

My legs ached from running. I had a sharp pain in my side. "If I remember the map, Goodbye Land is at the back of the park," I choked out. "Maybe there's an exit up there. Maybe we can escape HorrorLand."

I grabbed the sides of the ladder and climbed to the top. A door in the ceiling opened easily. I could see the sky above me. I scrambled out – on to grass. And held the door open for the others.

"We're out!" Carly Beth cried, pumping her fists in the air.

"We got away from those MPs," Robby said. He slapped me on the back. "That was *awesome*, Michael! Letting those beasts out of their cages – that was *genius*!"

I raised my face to the sun. The warmth felt really good. My heart was still pounding from our narrow escape. "Those gorilla creatures were real," I said. "They weren't pretend."

"How did they get down there?" Sheena asked, shaking her head. "Why do they keep them underground? What is *going on* here?"

"Let's just get out of the park," I said. "We can try to figure it out later."

"Do you really think there's an exit in Goodbye Land?" Billy asked.

"Only one way to find out," I said.

Goodbye Land stood behind a tall hedge. The hedge rose up way over our heads.

No way to climb it. I trotted along in its shadow, looking for an opening. Finally, I saw a tiny space.

I scrunched up my body. Turned sideways. And pushed myself through the hedge.

Brushing prickly needles off me, I gazed around. I was in a wide grassy park. A patch of tall trees threw a long shadow over the grass.

No people anywhere in sight. No Horrors or MPs.

A wide empty park.

I turned back to the hedge. Where were the others?

"Hey!" I opened my mouth to call to them.

But a hand wrapped around my mouth from behind. Then another hand wrapped around my waist – and dragged me into the trees.

The hands let go. I spun around – and stared at two gigantic Horrors.

I let out an angry *roar*. The monster in me took over. I balled my hands into tight fists. I got ready to attack them both.

"What's the *big idea*?" I screamed. "What do you think you're *doing*? My friends and I are Very Special Guests here. Have you all gone *crazy*?"

They both motioned for me to calm down. I read the name tags on the front of their purple uniforms. One was called Benson. The other was Clem.

"Easy, kid," Benson said. "No one is going to hurt you."

"Were you trying to leave? You *were* – weren't you!" Clem said. "We can't let you leave the park. You and your friends have to stay here."

"Why?" I yelled. "This is a free country! I can go anywhere I want!"

"You and your friends think you've figured everything out," Benson said. "But you don't know what you're doing."

"I know what I'm doing," I shot back. "I'm going to get my friends out of danger."

"Look, kid," Benson said. "We've had a few small problems here. I'll admit it. A few things went wrong."

"But we need you to stay here," his partner said. "Take it easy. Enjoy the park, Michael. And stop being such a troublemaker."

"No way!" I cried. "If you think I'm a troublemaker, too bad. Someone is out to get us here. Someone is trying to hurt us. And I'm going to get *out* of this park and take my friends with me. Then we're going to tell the whole world what goes on here."

They narrowed their eyes to slits. Their expressions turned angry. They took a few steps towards me.

I raised my fists and prepared to fight them.

But a third Horror suddenly appeared. "I'll handle this," he boomed. He waved Benson and Clem away. "You can go. I've got this kid."

This new Horror was tall and athletic-looking. He had short yellow horns on top of wavy green hair. His fat nose and tiny chin made him look a lot like a pug dog.

He waited for the other two to leave. Then he turned to me. I saw that he had taken off his name tag. "Michael," he said, "you want out of HorrorLand – don't you?"

I didn't answer his question. Instead, I took a few steps back. "Who are you?" I demanded. "Why did you take off your name tag? What are you planning to do to me?"

"I'm going to help you," he said softly. He pulled a small square mirror from his pocket. "You want to go, Michael. So I'm going to help you go."

"Huh?" I squinted at him. Then I gazed into the mirror.

I suddenly felt strange. Off-balance. I felt a strong pull from the mirror. As if I were being drawn to it by a powerful magnet.

"Go ahead," the Horror urged. "Don't fight it, Michael. You want to leave, remember? I'm helping you leave. Go with it. . . Go with it. . ."

His voice faded as I was pulled. . . pulled towards the glass. Pulled to my reflection in the little mirror.

So strange. . .

I could feel the smoothness of the glass . . . the cool liquid feel of it. . .

Deeper into the glass . . . deeper. And then *through* it!

Through the mirror.

A rush of cold air blew over me. It made me shut my eyes.

I felt myself falling. I struggled to catch my balance.

137

When I opened my eyes, the Horror...the trees...the grass...all had disappeared.

"Hey – where am I?" I cried out loud.

I gazed around. I was standing in a huge amusement park. But I didn't recognize anything.

I squinted, waiting for my eyes to focus. I saw roller coasters high in the sky. And a Ferris wheel with cars shaped like sharks and alligators.

And then...my eyes stopped at a red-and-white sign. It had big blood-red letters across it: PP.

PP? *Panic Park?*

Was this really Panic Park?

"Hey, I'm in Panic Park! I found it. I found Panic Park!" I shouted.

Then I felt a wave of fear slide over me.

I glanced around, my heart pounding. *But... where IS Panic Park?* I wondered. *And... how do I get back to my friends?*

To be continued in...

⑧ SAY CHEESE – AND DIE SCREAMING!

But first...

Before HorrorLand,
another monster starred in

BE CAREFUL WHAT YOU WISH FOR

Take a peek
at R.L. Stine's classic bone-chilling prequel.
Now available with exclusive
new bonus features –
including fortune-telling tools of the trade!

Having your breath knocked out has to be the worst feeling in the world. It's just so scary. You try to breathe, and you can't. And the pain just keeps swelling, like a balloon being blown up right inside your chest.

I really thought I was dead meat.

Of course I was perfectly OK a few minutes later. I still felt a little shaky, a little dizzy. But I was basically OK.

Ellen insisted that one of the girls walk me to the locker room. Naturally, Judith volunteered. As we walked, she apologized. She said it had been an accident. Totally an accident.

I didn't say anything. I didn't want her to apologize. I didn't want to talk to her at all. I just wanted to strangle her again.

This time for good.

I mean, how much can one girl take in a day? Judith had tripped me in maths class, dumped her disgusting tapioca pudding all over my new

Doc Martens in Home Ec., and kicked me unconscious in basketball practice.

Did I really have to smile and accept her apology now?

No way! No way in a million years.

I trudged silently to the locker room, my head bent, my eyes on the floor.

When she saw that I wasn't going to buy her cheap apology, Judith got angry. *Do you believe that?* She shoves her knee through my chest – then *she* gets angry!

"Why don't you just fly away, Byrd!" she muttered. Then she went trotting back to the gym floor.

I got changed without showering. Then I collected my stuff, slunk out of the building, and got my bike.

That's really the last straw, I thought, walking my bike across the car park behind school.

It was about half an hour later. The late afternoon sky was grey and overcast. I felt a few light drops of rain on my head.

The last straw, I repeated to myself.

I live two streets away from the school, but I didn't feel like going home. I felt like riding and riding and riding. I felt like just going straight and never turning back.

I was angry and upset and shaky. But mainly angry.

Ignoring the raindrops, I climbed on to my bike and began pedalling in the direction away from my house. Front gardens and houses went by in a whir. I didn't see them. I didn't see anything.

I pedalled harder and harder. It felt so good to get away from school. To get away from Judith.

The rain started to come down a little harder. I didn't mind. I raised my face to the sky as I pedalled. The raindrops felt cold and refreshing on my hot skin.

When I looked down, I saw that I had reached Jeffers' Woods, a long stretch of trees that divides my neighbourhood from the next.

A narrow bike path twisted through the tall, old trees, which were winter bare and looked sort of sad and lonely without their leaves. Sometimes I took the path, seeing how fast I could ride over its curves and bumps.

But the sky was darkening, the black clouds hovering lower. And I saw a glimmering streak of lightning in the sky over the trees.

I decided I'd better turn around and ride home.

But as I turned, someone stepped in front of me.

A woman!

I gasped, startled to see someone on this empty road by the woods.

I squinted at her as the rain began to fall harder, pattering on the pavement around me. She wasn't young, and she wasn't old. She had dark eyes, like two black pieces of coal, on a pale face. Her thick black hair flowed loosely behind her.

Her clothing was sort of old-fashioned. She had a bright red heavy woollen shawl pulled around her shoulders. She wore a long black skirt down to her ankles.

Her dark eyes seemed to light up as she met my stare.

She looked confused.

I should have run.

I should have pedalled away from her as fast as I could.

If only I had known. . .

But I didn't flee. I didn't escape.

Instead, I smiled at her. "Can I help you?" I asked.

MONSTERS WANTED

HorrorLand is looking for a few good monsters to operate our rides and attractions. If YOU are a monster, please fill out this form and send it to Les Chompem, Monster Relations.

Name: _____

Height: _____   Length of Horns: _____

Length of Tail: _____

Which of these creatures do you look like? Circle one.

   A giant insect

   An octopus

   A Komodo dragon

   All of the above

On a scale of 1 to 5, how ugly are you?

   1: A little Ugly

   2:

   3:

   4:

   5: Too Ugly to work anywhere else

FIND THE REST at
WWW.ESCAPEHorrorLAND.COM
—LIZZY

Connects to Map #9

Connects to Map # 5

About the Author

R.L. Stine's books are read all over the world. So far, his books have sold more than 300 million copies, making him one of the most popular children's authors in history. Besides Goosebumps, R.L. Stine has written the teen series Fear Street and the funny series Rotten School, as well as the Mostly Ghostly series, The Nightmare Room series, and the two-book thriller *Dangerous Girls*. R.L. Stine lives in New York with his wife, Jane, and Minnie, his King Charles spaniel. You can learn more about him at www.RLStine.com.

THIS BOOK IS YOUR TICKET TO

www.EnterHorrorLand.com

CHECKLIST #7

☑ AN ALL-NEW ALL-TERRIFYING SERIES FROM THE MASTER OF FRIGHT!

Goosebumps
HorrorLand

MY FRIENDS CALL ME MONSTER
R.L. STINE
SCHOLASTIC

☐ You're trapped in the Bat Barn. Ouch! Those bats have sharp claws! Can you stop this BAT-astrophe?

☐ Uh-oh! Here come the Monster Police! Don't fall into their trap!

☐ Search for the hidden stairway into the HorrorLand underground.

☐ Explore the tunnels beneath HorrorLand. Find the right door to escape the gorillas but be careful not to enter Panic Park...

☐ Danger! An 8-foot Horror awaits you! Can you defeat him before it's too late?

THE ORIGINAL SERIES FROM THE MASTER OF FRIGHT!

Goosebumps

BE CAREFUL WHAT YOU WISH FOR
R.L. STINE
SCHOLASTIC
NOW WITH BONUS FEATURES!

_____
USER NAME

_____
PASSWORD

NOW WITH BONUS FEATURES!

 SCHOLASTIC

SCHOLASTIC and associated logos are trademarks and/ or registered trademarks of Scholastic Inc.